BAD BEHAVIOR

JESSA JAMES

Bad Behavior: Copyright © 2020 by Jessa James

All Rights Reserved. No part of this book may be reproduced or transmitted in any form or by any means, electrical, digital or mechanical including but not limited to photocopying, recording, scanning or by any type of data storage and retrieval system without express, written permission from the author.

Published by Jessa James
James, Jessa
Bad Behavior

Cover design copyright 2020 by Jessa James, Author

Images/Photo Credit: Design Credit: BookCoverForYou

Publisher's Note:
This book was written for an adult audience. The book may contain explicit sexual content. Sexual activities included in this book are strictly fantasies intended for adults and any activities or risks taken by fictional characters within the story are neither endorsed nor encouraged by the author or publisher.

This book has been previously published.

GET A FREE BOOK!

Join my mailing list to be the first to know of new releases, free books, special prices and other author giveaways.

http://freehotcontemporary.com

PROLOGUE 1

1997, Redemption Beach High School

I'm walking along the cement breezeway between classes, examining the scuff marks on my ancient black Converse and listening to my friend Asher as he rattles on.

"The thing about my parents, is that they have a lot of money, but they're so stingy!" Asher says. "They wouldn't even let me go on that debate trip, because they said it wasn't a good use of money."

He rolls his eyes. I just nod. I've heard this story before, but I don't feel the need to stop him or tell him that. Besides, we're only a few minutes away from Ms. Harper's math class

Asher's always complaining about his parents, which makes sense, I guess. I mean, it's kind of hard to hear, since my parents ditched me and my two little brothers ages ago. Now we live with my Grandma Jane. She's nice and she means well, but she's also really *old*.

Three years ago, I attempted to have my first sleep over at Asher's place. Asher and I were only eleven, practically babies.

Asher's parents took one look at me and decided that I'm a bad influence. No amount of arguing or pleading on Asher's part would change their minds. They canceled the sleep over, and try to discourage us from hanging out anytime they can.

It's hard not to hate them for that.

I glance at Asher. With his ironed blue dress shirt and carefully pressed Chinos, he's pretty much the opposite of me. I'm wearing baggy jeans and a holey Nirvana t-shirt.

We are different in looks too, Asher with his blond hair smoothed back, me with my dark hair spiked up. I've always looked like a rebel, Asher has always looked like a choir boy.

That's how we became friends, actually. Asher was the new kid in school, and he was a prime target for the playground bullies. I looked dark and edgy. That was enough for most of the kids at school. They didn't want to mess with me.

I stepped in and kept him from getting his head dunked in the toilet. We've been friends ever since.

Asher elbows me in the side. "Don't you think?"

"Err… yeah. Totally," I say, even though I have no idea what he was talking about. I zoned out there, hard.

"I'm telling you, Zoe Waters got totally stacked over the summer break," Asher says.

I roll my eyes. The only thing Zoe Waters has done is to start wearing a bra. Other than that, she's as flat-chested as the rest of our ninth grade class. Believe me, I've looked.

We come up to the next building, the clear glass door only partially offsetting the fact that the ugly brown brick building practically eats all the sunlight. I swing the door open, holding it for Asher. Asher walks through, stopping just inside the door.

"Oof," I say, running into him. "Watch it, dude."

But Asher just gestures down the long hall, lined on both sides with lockers and classroom doors. At the other end Mr. Smith and Mrs. Song, the principal and school counselor, are walking straight toward us.

I glance around, wondering who is in trouble. I get nervous, even though I don't think there's anything I've done recently enough to worry.

"Hey, we better get going," I whisper to Asher. "Come on. Ms. Harper will count us as absent, for sure."

We start down the hall, but Mr. Smith spots us. An thin older man in black slacks and a pink and grey striped shirt, he looks at me with an intense expression. Ms. Song is a tiny, pretty blonde. She clasps her hands as we grow closer.

That can't be a good sign.

I glance at Asher, and see the same look on his face as is on my own. He's trying to figure out which one of us is in trouble with the principal.

"Mr. Hart?" Ms. Song says, her voice squeaky and chipmunk-like. "Could you come with me? I want to talk to you."

My stomach sinks. What did I do wrong this time? I wrack my brain, but come up empty.

Asher looks at me, conflicted. He's probably mentally wiping his brow, because it could've been either one of us that was in trouble.

"I should go to class, I guess," Asher says.

"Yeah. I'll catch up." I shift my back pack on my shoulder as Asher darts to the side of Mr. Smith and Ms. Song.

"Let's go," Ms. Song says. I think I hear a note of sadness in her voice, but I'm not sure. "Come to my office, please."

She turns and leads the way, her heels clicking on the tiled floor with each step. I am trying to think what this could be about. I've been hauled into the principal's office plenty of times, but never Ms. Song's office.

When we reach her office, not much bigger than a closet, she directs me to sit down in one of the orange bucket seats in front of her desk.

Mr. Smith closes the door behind us, then actually pats me on the shoulder, which makes me jump. I look up at him, startled.

"We have some hard news, son," he says, looking woeful. "Your grandmother has passed on. She's no longer with us."

My jaw drops open. I feel... odd. Mostly I'm thinking, *of all the things that he could've said, I was just not expecting that.*

"You mean... she's dead?" I manage.

Mr. Smith shoots Ms. Song a look, then nods to me. "I'm afraid so, yes. One of your neighbors found her. It looks like a heart attack."

I slouch a little. "What... what does that mean for us? Me and my little brothers, I mean. Why… I mean… where will I go after school?"

My voice cracks on the last word. All I can imagine is that I'm going to walk in the door of Grandma Jane's house, and she won't be there.

Fuck.

"Well, we've contacted the department of children and family services," Ms. Song says, coming over to put her hand on my shoulder.

"What? Why?" I ask, dazed.

"They will find a good place for you to stay tonight. And then they'll help you figure out what the next step will be," Mr. Smith says.

I look at him, my eyes starting to fill. "Are they the foster care people?"

I know all about foster care. Back when my mom abandoned us, until my grandma turned up, the three of us were in foster care for a few weeks. All of us were in different homes.

"Yes, exactly," Mr. Smith says.

"I'm not going with them," I utter, growing angry. My tears spill over, slowly leaking down my face. "They won't even put me and my brothers together."

"We should just see what they say," Ms. Song cuts in. "They know best, I'm sure."

I can imagine my brothers now. I can see Forest being told about Grandma Jane, Gunnar being told that we're going to different foster care homes.

Gunnar is so young, he won't even remember me and Forest after a few months.

I clench my fists, standing up so abruptly that my chair tips over.

"Oh, Jameson—" Ms. Song says.

"Hold on there, son." Mr. Smith grabs me by the arm. "You're going to have to wait here for a while. The people from DFACS should be here soon."

Tears are streaming down my face now, snot is oozing from

my nose. "No, you don't understand! I can't go into foster care! I need my brothers to stay with me!"

"Son—"

"Fuck you! Don't call me that!" I scream. But despite his age, Mr. Smith is still stronger than me. He manages to wrap his arms around me, pulling me deeper into the office.

"It's okay," he says.

"No it's not! You just told me my fucking grandma is dead!"

I'm hysterical, clawing at him, grabbing fistfuls of his pink and grey shirt, but he doesn't let go. Instead, he just tells me it's okay, over and over again.

But I know that it's not.

It's not okay.

My grandma is dead. My little brothers probably don't even know yet, but her death marks a turning point in our lives. I know that DFACS will probably try to force me and my brothers into separate foster homes.

Already, I'm scrambling to figure out the details of running away, to make it on my own. Not just me, but my two little brothers, too. Life has taken enough from us, I'll be damned if I let anyone split us up.

So no, nothing is okay. And I don't know if it ever will be again.

PROLOGUE 2

One Year Ago — Asher's Engagement Party

"And that's why I make a toast, here at the engagement party. To the happy couple!" Gunnar yells to the assembled crowd standing at the bar. I stand with my arm around my fiancée Jenna, smiling. My expression isn't fake, but it is strained. It's always a little weird to be the one toasted. "May you two live a long and happy life."

Everyone says "hear, hear!" or "cheers!" and lifts their glasses. I raise my glass of champagne, making eye contact with Jameson, who is skulking over in the corner. He looks tall and brooding in his dark jeans and leather jacket, which is kind of his thing.

Cece, Jameson's grungy surfer flavor of the week, downs her whole glass of champagne in one swallow. I personally can't stand the bottle blonde, do-I-have-to-wear-shoes-here thing, but to each his own I guess.

He inclines his head towards me, then takes a sip. Jameson has been a serious prick about my engagement to Jenna, so the fact that he was even invited here tonight is a gift from me to him.

I sip my champagne, turning away from him. It made me uneasy to have these feelings about Jameson, who has been my best friend since we were kids.

"Honey," Jenna says, handing me her champagne glass. She picks a little invisible speck of lint off of my white button down, smiling. "Could you get me another glass?"

"Sure. I could use something stronger, anyway."

"Just be sure not to get drunk." She straightens her black mini dress and flips her blonde hair. "I wouldn't want people to get the wrong impression of you."

"Heaven forbid," I say, rolling my eyes.

"I'm serious! There are a lot of people here tonight, not just your grubby friends."

I'm mildly offended, but glancing over at Jameson and his girlfriend, I can't really say anything. They are making out now, Cece fisting his leather jacket and pulling him down to her level. Soon enough, they'll disappear from the party for a while, probably to fuck in a closet somewhere.

I glance at Jenna, who has turned away. I'm almost jealous of Jameson in that regard. Jenna is an ice princess on her best day. But she also happens to be from a family that is wealthier than my family, and my family has money.

The fact that I bagged Jenna, and did it without their help, probably eats my mother and father up at night. That alone is worth ten Ceces, in my opinion.

I turn and head for the bar. The bartender goes to get my drinks, and I'm impressed by how efficiently he moves. Of course he does, I think. Jameson picked this place. Other than surfing, bartending is the only passion Jameson probably has.

Well, that and grimy former strippers.

Still, as I look around at the liquor bottles lined up so neatly, at the bartenders doing their job very diligently, I find myself jealous. If I knew anything about liquor, I would set up a bar in a heartbeat.

I even have a trust fund, set up by my grandparents. I've never touched it, afraid to spend even a cent of that money.

I sigh, looking to my right. My little sister Emma is sitting on a barstool at the end of the bar, staring off into space. I look in the general direction that she's staring, but I just see Jameson and Cece making out.

My eyes linger on Jameson, and I remember my moment of longing. I have a lightbulb moment, of sorts. A fission of energy passes through me, setting my mind on fire.

I could have a bar like this one. Hell, with Jameson's knowledge and my business prowess, I feel like we could really make something great.

I hesitate, because Jameson has really been a pain in the ass lately about Jenna. He's been grouchy and downright antagonistic about her, which has led to icy silences and pouting from her side.

But the idea of running a bar with Jameson is so great; him carefully crafting the perfect old fashioned, me handling the day to day worries and the money.

The idea is too appealing to pass up. At the very least, I have to tell him about it.

I move swiftly, my mind made up. I get waylaid by a couple of Jenna's friends before I can talk to him, of course. But I track him down eventually, before he can make his exit with Cece.

"Hey. You got a minute?" I say.

He swirls the whiskey in his glass and looks at me with amusement. "This whole party is for you. Of course I have a minute."

"You wanna go outside?" I ask.

Jameson nods and tells Cece he'll be back. I lead the way to the door, pushing it open. I step out of the air conditioning, trading it for the early evening sea breeze. We're only a few blocks away from the ocean right now, if the tang of salt in the air didn't give it away.

I lean up against the rough wood wall of the bar, and Jameson does the same. We both look out at the street while I gather my thoughts.

To my surprise, Jameson speaks first.

"Is this about Jenna?" he asks.

I look at him. He isn't showing any emotion, but he must be all wound up inside if he thinks I called him out here for a showdown.

"No." I make my word quick and vehement, so he knows I'm

serious. "I mean, lay off Jenna. But no, this is something different."

His brow knits together as he tries to suss out what I mean. He doesn't say anything though, so I continue.

"I think we should start a bar."

His expression of puzzlement is priceless. "You... what?"

"A bar. You set the menu, I handle the money. We both have a say in the atmosphere. Hell, I think your brothers can help run it."

"What are you fucking talking about?" He turns to me, leaning on the wall.

"I just had this moment, this sort of inspired moment. I was sipping a drink inside, and I thought... we can do this better. I thought, 'Jameson and I could really crush it if we had a bar'."

Jameson looks at me like I might have a head injury.

"You are saying... you were standing at the bar, having what I suppose was a less than stellar drink... and it made you think that we should run our own place??" He looks totally thrown.

"Yeah, man. I have the money. You have the skills..."

He rubs a hand over his face. "I'm at the first job that I've worked for more than a year."

"You've been there for like four years."

"Yeah, and I only remember two of them. The first two were consumed by whiskey and cocaine. Even now, I still can't stop wanting to fuck every hot chick that walks in the door."

I grin. "Yeah, yeah. Convince me that you're not the perfect guy to open a restaurant with. And what about Cece?"

He frowns. "What about her?"

"I thought she was... nice. And that you guys had a connection, or whatever." My lack of sincerity shows, and he rolls his eyes.

"What about you?" Jameson asks. "You've never made anything more complex than a rum and coke. You've never been in the service industry. You've never managed anyone..."

"That's not true!" I chip in. "What about—"

"If you bring up the summer before eighth grade right now, I swear I'm leaving," he threatens. He knows me too well.

"Just think about what our bar would be like," I say, switching topics. "We'd find a place on the beach. You could serve shit in fancy glasses, which you're always going on about—"

"Not everything needs to be served in a tumbler," he mutters.

"You could put on good music, turn down the lights, and schmooze your way into the heart of any girl there with just one line." I wiggle my brows for comedic effect. "All you'd have to say is that you're the owner."

That appears to give him pause. He rubs the back of his neck, but continues frowning. I'm used to that expression, though.

"I don't know," he finally says. "It seems like a really bad idea."

"But…?"

"That's it."

"You know, I'm going to roll with it. I think you're more intrigued than you let on."

He just squints at me silently. I reach out and clap him on the shoulder.

"You just wait," I promise. "It's going to be great."

Jameson just shakes his head. "Can I buy you a drink, at least?"

"That you can, man. That you can."

Turning my back on the sultry evening, I head inside.

PROLOGUE 3

Four Months Ago — CURE Bar

"Hey Emma, what do you think?" Jameson asks, scratching his stubbled cheek.

The wall behind the bar is lit up by glowing neon string lights, and it showcases the hundred or so brands of liquor that Jameson insisted on. He stands back, admiring his handiwork. I think that it's absolutely amazing, but then again I think that almost everything Jameson touches is amazing.

"Uhhh, it looks great," I say from my seat at the bar. I'm taking up all the space by spreading out my law school books, but I'm not studying law. Instead, I'm studying Jameson. "Maybe you should add another bottle over there on the right?"

I point to a spot. He looks at where I'm pointing, nodding slowly. "Good eye. It looks totally bare in that spot."

He grabs another bottle, reaching up to put it in the bare spot. I bite my lip. Jameson looks ridiculously good right now, just in dark jeans that hug his ass just so, a black NIN t-shirt, and blood red Chucks.

"It looks good," I say, my cheeks turning red even as I say it. By it, I mean every inch of him... and by good, I mean *appetizing*, *enticing*, and *tempting to the extreme*.

I sigh. Forest comes out of the back room, looking suave as ever in a green sweater and jeans. His dark hair and beard look pretty alluring; if I wasn't already so infatuated with Jameson I would probably have a thing for Forest.

He pulls his fiancée Addison along by the wrist. She doesn't say anything, just looks good in her pristine white dress, her hair artfullypinned up.

"Hey guys," Forest says.

"Finish checking out the liquor cave that I built upstairs?" Jameson asks Forest.

"Yeah. It's kind of trippy to see several thousand dollars of booze in one location. But it looks like everything is ready for the opening tomorrow."

"Right on. What time will you be here tomorrow?"

Forest glances at Addison. "What time do you think we'll be done with brunch with your parents? Around four? "

She inclines her head ever so slightly, which I guess means that she approves. I wonder what her deal is. It's not exactly an ice vibe I get from her, like I feel with Asher's fiancee Jenna. I just don't get anything from Addison.

It's very weird.

I turn my head as Gunnar bursts in the front door, three pretty blondes dressed to the nines in tow. For his part, Gunnar looks like he just left a dance club, because of the way he's dressed in a black checked dress shirt that's partially unbuttoned and a pair of black jeans.

He's obviously just said something funny, because they are all laughing.

"Ladies, just sit over there if you will," he says, pointing to one of the booths. He winks at them. "I just need to be here for a minute, and then we can go back to my place."

My eyebrows rise, but the girls just titter. Gunnar turns his attention to me, walking toward the bar. "Emma. Looking good, as usual."

I squirm a little under his gaze. Gunnar is a complete tool, but damn if he's not good looking enough to pull it off.

"Uh, thanks," I manage.

"Hey," Jameson says, scowling. "You know the rules. No hitting on Emma. Same rules for everybody."

I turn bright red and wish I could sink down into my seat. Asher has been announcing the same rule ever since I was old enough to put on a training bra. It's super humiliating.

"I was just commenting," Gunnar says with a shrug. He notices Forest and Addison. "What's up?"

Forest crosses his arms. "We were supposed to meet here over an hour ago. Asher already came and left."

Gunnar rolls his eyes. "I'm here. I didn't realize you would make it into a big deal."

"It is a big deal," Jameson jumps in and corrects him. "How are we supposed to have fucking employees show up on time if we just show up whenever we feel like it?"

"Mea culpa," Gunnar says, but he doesn't really look very sorry. "What am I supposed to be doing here, anyway?"

Jameson's jaw clenches. Forest steps in for him. "Can you just go upstairs and check on everything? Make sure that all the rum and tequila and mezcal and pisco you asked for is in stock."

"Aye aye," Gunnar says. He disappears into the back room.

"Every time he starts telling me how I'm too uptight, I'm this close to punching him in the fucking face," Jameson declares, turning back to the bar.

The front door opens again, and a gorgeous young Asian woman with long hair and porcelain skin sticks her head in. When she sees Forest and Jameson, she brightens and enters. I look longingly at her short denim shorts and her oversized blue tank top.

If my parents saw me out and about in an outfit like that, they'd flip. Hell, I think that Asher would even frog march me back home to change if he saw me wearing that... and he's supposed to be the young, cool rebel of our uptight family.

"Hi," she says, waving a sheaf of papers. To my surprise, she has a posh British accent. "I just brought the rest of my documents. I hope I'm not interrupting anything?"

I look at Forest, whose mouth has sort of fallen open. He is blatantly checking this woman out, rather than rushing to take the papers from her. Addison just looks on; whatever she feels is certainly not showing on the outside.

"Maia, hey," Jameson calls, making his way out from behind the bar. "I'll take whatever you've got."

Maia hands him the papers, smiling at me. She extends her hand to me. "I don't believe we've met. I'm Maia Yu. I'll be waiting tables here."

I take her hand. "Emma Alderisi. I don't work here, I just hang out."

"It's a pleasure to meet you. And I don't believe we've met?" she says, turning to Addison.

"Addison Raven," she replies, crossing her arms. "I'm marrying Forest."

Maia looks to Forest, who has closed his mouth but continues to look at her with something akin to awe.

Jameson clears his throat. "Forest was just leaving. Isn't that right?"

Forest's dirty look at Jameson is unmistakable. "Yeah. I'll see you guys later."

He leads his pretty wife-to-be out of the bar. Maia turns and glances at the blonde girls sitting in one of the booths, absorbed in their phones.

"Are you still hiring?" Maia asks, puzzled. I snicker.

"Jesus, no," Jameson says. "They are waiting on my other brother…"

"What's that now?" Gunnar says, popping out of the back room. He takes one look at Maia and turns up his charm to a ten. "Hey. We haven't met. I'm Gunnar."

"Maia." She shakes his hand. He holds onto it for a second too long, but she is too classy to act like it bothered her. She tosses her hair, unruffled. "If that's it, I'll go. You need us back here tomorrow at three, right?"

"Yes," Jameson and Gunnar say at once. Jameson shoots Gunnar a dirty look. Gunnar grins back, unabashed.

"See you tomorrow," Jameson says.

"We should go too, girls," Gunnar says, walking over to them. "Maia, we are all just going to my place for a drink…"

"Leave her alone, Gunnar," Jameson growls. "Maia, see you later."

"Later." Maia wiggles her fingers and leaves. Gunnar starts after her, although I doubt that he knows exactly what he's going to do when he catches up to her.

"Gunnar," Jameson says threateningly. Gunnar slows, then looks at the three blondes, his shoulders slumping a little.

"Let's go," he says, waiting for the three girls to get up and make their way to the door. He looks back. "Bye, Emma."

I wave, my cheeks going pink. Gunnar is definitely not my type, but he is ridiculously handsome. Not to mention a terrible flirt.

Jameson puts the paperwork on the bar, then returns to looking at the back wall. "You know what this needs?"

I cock my head. "No, what?"

"Some flowers," he says, squinting up at the top shelf. "Like some of the dried flowers that the interior decorator brought, in empty liquor bottles."

He goes into the back room, reappearing with a couple of stacked cardboard boxes. He comes over to the bar. "Do you mind?"

I pick up my law textbooks that I have scattered all around, shoving them to one side. "Nah. I'm not really even working anyway."

Jameson chuckles as he opens one of the boxes. The first box contains empty liquor bottles, the labels on some of them so old that they're starting to peel off. The second box is filled with dried flowers, mostly lavender and baby's breath.

"Ooooh, these look great," I say as he starts to lay set them out on the counter. "Can I help?"

"Sure. Thanks." He says it kind of gruffly, but it still makes me blush.

I pick up a few of both kinds of flower, sticking them into the neck of the first bottle. I glance at him. "Like this?"

He looks thoughtful, and grabs a little more baby's breath. "Maybe just a few more…"

He leans over, reaching across me to put them in the bottle. He's suddenly really close, close enough that I can smell the scent of soap and leather on him. Goosebumps suddenly break out all over my arms, even though he's not touching me.

I notice a couple of black lines peeking out of the neck of his shirt, leading down to… something. I didn't know that Jameson had tattoos, but of course it makes sense. It fits right in with his brooding bad boy persona, if you ask me.

Plus

"Does this look good?" he asks, arranging the stems.

"What?" I ask vacantly. It takes some effort to rip my eyes from his muscular body. "Oh, uh. Yeah, totally."

He shoots me a look, but doesn't say anything. "If you want to do a few bottles, I'll put them up over on the back wall."

I bite my lip, nodding. I start to arrange another bunch, reaching for an empty bottle. He grabs the one he finished and starts trying it out different places among the full liquor bottles on the wall.

"This is really a smart idea," I say to him.

"It's funny to hear you say that, being that you're in law school," he says.

I frown, pausing. "That doesn't mean that you can't have a stroke of genius."

Jameson glances back at me for a second, shaking his head a little.

"Are you serious? I definitely dumped a girl last week because she told me that I'm not very bright." He frowns with concentration, replacing one of the bottles on the lower left. "What do you think about that? Maybe we could do six or seven bottles like that?"

"Wait, what? A girl told you you're not very bright?" I ask, shocked.

"Yeah. I mean… I told her that I dropped out of my first year of high school to take care of Forest and Gunnar, and she goes, 'That makes sense. It's okay, I'm not dating you for your brain.'"

My jaw drops. "That's not fair!"

He turns and looks at me. "It's nothing to get upset over."

"It is! She sounds like a bitch." I put on an exaggerated pout.

His eyes crinkle with humor. "You're cute when you're all worked up."

I turn beet red for about the thousandth time today. "I'm just stating facts," I mumble, embarrassed. Luckily, the moment passes, and I go back to arranging flowers in their makeshift vases.

Jameson puts a couple more bottles up, then pauses, stroking his stubbled chin. "I don't think I can reach any higher. How do you feel about climbing up to stand on the shelf here?"

I raise my eyebrows. "Ummm..."

He pats the back shelf. "I mean, I'd help you get up and down. I promise not to look up your dress or anything."

I imagine the kind of help he means, which would probably involve a lot of close contact. I push up out of my seat.

"Sure."

"Alright, come here," he instructs, looking at the wall. "I'll boost you up."

I do as he says, taking his hands. I feel weird, doing a physical activity in my tiny pale green sundress. I blush again. The feel of his hands on my body is absolutely sinful, though there's nothing sinful about what we're doing.

Jameson's so much warmer than I am, just by nature. I take a deep breath, inhaling his clean scent. He grabs me by the waist, pushing me up, until I can stand on the shelf.

At some point in the transaction, he pushes my actual ass up with one big hand. I can't help the nervous laughter that escapes me.

"Are you steady?" he asks.

"I think so—" I say. Then I squeak as I fall backwards.

Shit shit shit shit— I definitely expect to hit the ground, *hard*.

But then I land in Jameson's arms, as perfectly as I could've dreamed. Our faces are so close just then, his eyes on my face. All I can think of is that I am surely going to drown in his dark gaze.

His eyes dip down to my mouth. I swear, the whole world around us slows. I lick my bottom lip, suddenly more certain than anything that he's about to kiss me.

Yes. It's happening. My eyelids start to flutter closed, in preparation.

"Whoa!" Asher's voice throws me for a loop. I open my eyes to see him coming in through the front door. Jameson hastily puts me down, moving to step away from me. "What's going on?"

"I fell!" I blurt out, not wanting Jameson to get in trouble with Asher. "I was trying to reach something. Jameson just caught me, is all."

"Relax," Asher says, coming up behind the bar. "Jameson knows the rule. Don't you, Jay?"

Jameson is slightly red-faced. "Yep. Emma is off limits."

I grimace at his words. Yeah, yeah, they've been saying the exact same thing ever since I turned thirteen.

"That's right," Asher says, clapping him on the back.

Jameson looks so guilty, I almost feel bad for him. That is, until he speaks.

"I would never do that to you," he says to Asher. Then he looks me right in the eye. "Never."

My cheeks start to burn, and I clench my jaw. "I'm not a little girl, Asher. I can make decisions for myself."

Asher and J both look at me. Asher snorts. "Not with my friends, you can't. Isn't that right, J?"

There's a few seconds of silence. I look at J, at the conflicted expression on his face. I begin to feel a tiny flicker of hope. Is he about to stand up for me?

God, is he about to tell Asher that he has feelings for me? My heart skips a beat.

But of course, he doesn't. He probably doesn't even feel anything for me, because his next words cut pretty deeply.

"Your friends are off limits for a reason," J says to Asher, casting his glance downward. "Besides, I wouldn't ever do anything with *Emma*. She's so... *young*."

Oh, no he didn't. J definitely just spoke to Asher about me, like I'm not here. I grind my teeth.

"I'm right here!" I say angrily, waving my hand. "I don't like being talked about like I'm not in the room."

J just continues to look away, like I have never existed. I could smack him, I'm so mad.

Asher looks at me with an impatient expression. "You're here *and* you're snippy. Hooray for us."

"Fuck you," I say through gritted teeth. I'm humiliated right now, and it is definitely their fault. "Both of you can go to hell."

"Emma—" Asher says, rolling his eyes.

That's it. Asher's eye roll is the nail in the coffin for me. I hate both of them right now.

"I'm going to go home. At least Evie appreciates me as a roommate… and as an adult," I hiss. I stomp around the bar, feeling like they made me act childishly. I jam my textbooks into my satchel, fuming.

I'm angry at Asher, yes. He needs to let me grow up.

But more than that, I'm angry at J. I feel like he just looked me in the eye and said those things to be hurtful. That makes him an asshole, no matter how you slice it.

"Emma, don't be like that," Jameson says as I shoulder my bag. I shoot him a glare.

"Piss off," I say, storming off toward the door.

I leave them there behind the bar, shaking their heads. Pushing open the door, I step out into the bright afternoon light. I'm furious at both of them, shaking a little.

Asher can go put all that stuff about me being his baby sister where the sun don't shine. And Jameson?

Jameson seems so manly and grown, except where Asher is concerned. He needs to grow up, and grow a pair. No matter how attractive Jameson may be, I don't have time for anybody that doesn't want me.

I just have to keep reminding myself of that… forever.

Grimacing, I start to walk home.

4

JAMESON

*G*etting caught in the back room of Cure, kissing my best friend's wife-to-be at their wedding rehearsal after party... let's just say it was not a part of my plan.

The night starts off with the pop of champagne corks flying around behind the bar. The lights are turned way down, and a playlist of Purity Ring remixes is playing loudly over the sound system. The doors to the outside are thrown open, letting in the salty air and the sound of the ocean waves of Redemption Beach crashing in the distance.

People are toasting the happy couple. It's a little premature if you ask me, but no one did. So I just keep my trap shut and work the bar. Behind the bar, I'm still the bartender, the master of my little domain.

On the floor of the restaurant, I would have to rub elbows with hedge fund managers and CEOs and Instagram models. The kind of people who went to expensive private colleges and talk about where they're *summering*. Not my crowd.

They're all here for Asher and his well-to-do fiancee Jenna. And I'm here too, me and the other Hart brothers. We're standing in for Asher's family, because they don't care about him and because we do.

Tonight is all for Asher. I just have to keep that in mind.

Really, it's okay to be around the Youtube starlets and tennis pros, because most of them think I'm just the help. They probably don't know that Asher and I even own this bar together.

Which is more than fine by me.

Not for the first time tonight, I wish I was at the beach, running out toward the water with a surf board under one arm. Actually, I am longing to be anywhere but here right now.

But I'm not. I'm here. I need to be useful, taking orders and making drinks. Otherwise, I turn into a pouty, angry man-child. Nobody wants that, especially not tonight.

I'm standing behind the bar, a bar towel slung over my shoulder, staring down the crowd of wedding guests with a not-quite-scowl. I consider whether I should put up glasses of water on the bar for the crowd or not. The party is definitely a success, meaning that almost everybody is a little drunk by now.

I have even been dipping into the expensive bourbons, a practice I frown upon for the other bartenders. But tonight is a party, a celebration of sorts. Even if I don't like what people are celebrating, I still have to be here.

Maia, a cute Asian girl who makes a hell of a Sazerac, drops her tray on the bar. She pulls her skintight black cocktail dress down a little.

"Jameson! Pop one of the bottles of rosé bubbly, will you?" she says, her upperclass British accent making *bubbly* sound refined.

I raise a questioning brow at her. "Why?"

"The bride to be wants 'something pink with bubbles'," she says with a shrug. "I'm a server. She gives me an order, I come and ask for it. You pour the drinks. That's usually how it works, anyway."

She gives me a look, like she knows exactly what I've been thinking, and she doesn't approve.

"Mmmph," I respond grumpily. Sparkling rosé isn't on the menu tonight, but I do as requested. It is for Asher, after all.

"Do you mind getting some champagne flutes down for me while you're at it, boss?" she asks, giving me a saccharine smile. "You're a million miles taller than me."

"I'm six foot three," I correct her. "You're just really short."

She sticks her tongue out at me, and I chuckle. I fetch a case of the glasses she wants off the back wall, setting it down on the bar.

I turn around to the towering neon-lit wall of different kinds of liquor. They're all grouped by type: whiskeys and bourbons together, vodkas and gins and aquavits, rums and tequilas and mezcals, piscos and brandies, and a few dozen bottles of wine.

We're at Cure, the bar that I co-own with my best friend Asher and my two brothers, Gunnar and Forest. At the moment, Cure is closed to the public for Asher's wedding party. Forty or so tipsy wedding guests, all gathered here on the night before the wedding.

It makes sense, as far as gathering places go.

After all, Cure was Asher's idea in the first place. He'll be the first one of the four of us to get married. I should be happy for him, but I'm not. I fucking hate his fiancee Jenna, and I think he can do way better than her.

But I swallow my words. The time come and gone to get all my thoughts and opinions about Jenna and the wedding out. I said my piece. Asher called me a prick.

And I am, without a doubt. A fuck up, a misanthrope, an anti-social brooder for whom opening this bar was a total shot in the dark. This bar, raising my little brothers, and keeping my friendship with Asher are really the only good things I've ever done.

God knows, if there was a cosmic accounting of my whole life, there are plenty of bad things in my past that tip the scale in favor of my being a total piece of shit. Like dropping out of school young, dating an endless stream of surfer chicks and pretty bar patrons, constantly partying, and wrecking not one but two motorcycles in my twenties.

I know that my past and my tendency toward gloom don't exactly make me lovable. I'm working on redemption, slowly.

I dip below the bar, to the low-boy coolers where the bottles of white and sparkling are kept. I search for a second, then find the right bottle. The rest is all muscle memory, peeling the foil off and unwinding the metal cage. I pop the bottle with as little fuss as possible, eyeing my brother Gunnar as I pour the bubbly into champagne flutes that I have set up on the bar.

Gunnar is next to me at the bar, pouring vodka and a little bit of cinnamon shrub together into a cocktail shaker. There are a whole line of pretty girls waiting for the shots that he's making. I clear my throat and send him a look.

Don't keep feeding the girls vodka, the look says. *Seriously.*

He grins and winks at me, then yells at the girls to bend backward over the marble-topped bar in order to receive their shots. Of course they do, giggling.

I can't roll my eyes hard enough. I put the champagne flutes onto the tray that Maia dropped. She scoops it up with a fake smile, carrying it off to the bride.

She doesn't like Jenna, either. Asher is the only one of the staff that Jenna is nice to. The rest of us are considered less than human.

I look across the bar to the booth where Jenna is ensconced with her whole rich, snobby clique. I watch Maia deliver the sparkling wine to Jenna's table, where beautiful ice queen Jenna is telling a story.

I see Jenna push her empty glass toward Maia without a thought. The music in here is too loud to know what Jenna is saying, but one look at her ruddy cheeks and her exultant expression as she talks to the people clustered around her...

Yeah, she is drunk. Not just drunk, but demanding. She downs the sparkling wine in two swallows, then holds the glass out to Maia to refill.

Again, she's not making eye contact. Jenna's too busy loudly telling her story. Everyone at her table laughs at once, and she looks right at home, basking in their adulation.

Maia takes the champagne flute, and heads towards another table to check that they don't need anything.

I grit my teeth. You would think that Maia really was just an unknown face, a server at some restaurant... but really, Asher and Jenna have been together since this place opened. Maia was our second employee.

Simply put, they know each other.

We should've hired catering staff to work this party, I think. That way everyone could mingle. And the staff could avoid Jenna's table…

I turn away and bite my tongue. When Maia comes back, I'll tell her she doesn't have to wait on Jenna anymore. I'll do it.

Things have been more than a little uneasy between Asher and me for the last few weeks, ever since I told him how I feel. Even though we've been best friends for almost twenty years, shit got awkward as fuck the second the words were out of my mouth.

Now we're here. Asher is schmoozing Jenna's parents over by the door to the patio, looking as golden as I am dark. In his checked shirt and khakis, he is exactly the guy you would want your princess-daughter to marry.

I swear to god, I can see his teeth sparkle from across the fucking room every time he laughs. Asher's almost a goddamned Disney prince, my diametric opposite.

I remember that I'm supposed to be throwing this party for him, and keep my thoughts about Jenna to myself.

"Hey," a voice says. I turn away from Asher to find his little sister Emma sliding into a seat at the bar.

Emma is twenty four, with her raven-colored hair done in a fancy updo, and she's wearing a pale pink body con dress like it's her *job*.

I'm not stupid enough to act like I know, though. I've been careful not to notice her for the last six years. She's the rich princess that wants for nothing. I may be a lot of things, but I'm definitely not her speed, and she's not mine. There are plenty of reasons why a guy like me shouldn't even *look* at someone like her.

For one thing, Emma's way younger than me. For another, she's what you could describe as perky. As the loner who stands behind the bar and broods, I'm definitely not into her animated attitude.

Then there's the fact that she's going to law school, whereas I dropped out of high school. We are worlds apart in that respect.

Plus, if Asher ever found out that I'd had so much as an impure thought about his little sister, he would have a fucking stroke. And then he'd murder me.

That would be a sad way to go.

I glower at Emma. "Aren't you supposed to be socializing? You know, representing your snooty-ass family, seeing as they can't be bothered to show their faces?"

Emma grins at me, her green eyes twinkling with delight. That's what I mean about *perky*. I refuse to let my eyes dip lower to check out her tits... but I'm sure they're perky too.

"My parents are absolutely *horrified* that Asher has found himself a girlfriend that isn't a social outcast. They're positively fuming that he did well for himself without any help from them. So I'm not representing them, no." She leans closer to me, biting her lower lip suggestively. "What have you got back there that's not wine?"

Don't look down at her tits. Don't look down at her tits, I tell myself. Then I look down at her tits anyway, small but perfect, pushed up by her dress.

I jerk my eyes away as soon as I realize that I'm doing it. Fucking hell. The last thing I need is for Emma to think that I'm a fucking pervert.

I make eye contact with her, and hesitate. There are plenty of pickup lines that float to the surface, but I ignore them.

"What kind of liquor do you want?" I ask, turning and picking up a metal cocktail shaker.

"Mmm..." she says, twisting a loop of her dark hair around a finger. "Vodka? I want something that doesn't taste like alcohol."

I make a noise of displeasure. Emma cocks her head at me.

"You asked what I wanted!" she says. "I want something sweet."

I shake my head and grab the vodka, pouring it in the cocktail shaker. "You like lemonade?"

"Who doesn't?" she asks.

I mix freshly squeezed lemon juice and a little homemade simple syrup into the tin, add a handful of ice cubes, then shake it. I pour it all into a highball glass, then top it off with a drizzle of fresh raspberry puree. I stick a straw in it, pulling a little of the concoction into the straw, and then pull the straw out for a taste.

Lemon and sugar hit my palate long before the vodka does. I wrinkle my nose at the sweetness. Perfect for her, though. When I serve it to her with a new straw, her eyes light up.

"Ooooh," she says. "It's pretty."

"Yup," I say, setting about washing my shaker out.

Emma sips the cocktail, her elbows on the bar. "This is amazing! What do you call it?"

I eye her. "The schoolgirl special," I reply dryly.

She blushes, her cheeks turning a shade darker than her pink dress. "You're the *actual* worst."

That makes me grin. "You'd do best to remember that."

I wink at her, and she rolls her eyes. "Thanks for the drink."

She picks up her cocktail and walks away, hips swaying. I watch her walk away for a few seconds, my mouth a little dry.

"Seriously?" my brother Forest says, coming up beside me behind the bar. Forest is the middle brother. He's as dressed up as I am dressed down, wearing dark slacks and a white button up. His dark hair is clipped close to his scalp, not almost-too-long and messy like mine is.

I yank my gaze away from her, glancing down at my black t-shirt and black jeans instead. Forest isn't done, though. "There are so many hot girls here, and you're staring at Emma? What is wrong with you?"

He's not wrong. At thirty three, I should definitely not be looking at someone almost a decade younger than me. I clear my throat and shake my head.

"Because I'm a dirty old man. Speaking of people who are too young for us, where's Addison tonight?" I ask, changing the subject.

He frowns and turns a little, pointing out his fiancee to me. A very thin redhead in a red silk dress, she's in a little group of women standing by the front door.

"Right there. And she's not too young for me. She's very

mature for her age." He reaches into the lowboy coolers under the bar and gets a beer, popping the cap off.

"Uh huh," I say. I lean back against the bar. "I seem to remember being invited to her twenty first birthday party last month."

"Fuck off," Forest says, pulling a face. He takes a sip of his beer. "You're just jealous."

"Of Addison? She's so controlling, dude. That's your thing, not mine."

Now he really glares at me. "Again, fuck off. Also, Asher asked me to remind you to keep everybody hydrated. Nobody wants to see Jenna toss her cookies during the wedding procession tomorrow."

I glance over at Jenna, and see her pantomiming something that looks an awful lot like sucking a huge dick. Everyone around her laughs, and she knocks back another glass of pink bubbles.

A sense of loathing rises in me. *Really, Asher?* I think. *That's who you're going to tie yourself to for the rest of your life?*

Forest laughs at my expression and claps me on the shoulder. "You have got to learn to mask your expressions better, J."

"I just don't see what Asher sees in her," I lament.

"And yet, here you are, working their rehearsal dinner reception," Forest says. I see Addison turn her head, looking for Forest. He sees it too, and sighs. "Alright. I've gotta get back to the conversation. Don't forget the water, though."

"Yeah," I say to his back as he heads over to his fiancee's side. "Right."

I think about the cases of bottled water that we have. I'd have to go upstairs to get them, up the creaky ass stairs and into the dusty little stock room, but then people would be able to take them to go. I head into the private back room that doubles as an office, and then up the stairs.

Grabbing two cases of water, I head back down. Except this time when I get back into the office, I am not alone.

Jenna is there, dressed in a white silk gown, and she is drunk off her ass. "Heyyyyy, there you are," she purrs.

I raise my brows. "You're looking for me?"

"Yeah," she says, coming closer. I can actually smell the wine on her breath, which is saying something, since wine usually isn't that strong. She staggers a little. "I want you to help me with my dress."

"Okay, hold on," I say, setting the waters on the desk. "Don't you want Asher to help you?"

"No!" she yells, turning around. Jesus, she's really drunk. She pulls her blonde hair over her shoulder. I look at her back, and I can see that her dress has split in a couple of places along the back zipper. "He can't see me like this!"

"Okay…" I say, frowning. "I don't know that I can fix it, though."

She starts unzipping the dress, stumbling over her own feet. "Get it off!"

"Just wait a second—" I start. She trips and starts to fall.

"Wha—" she begins to wail.

Hatred or no, I step forward and try to catch her. It's just ingrained in me, like muscle memory. I grab her, whipping her around.

Jenna, drunk as she is, starts laughing, blowing her wine breath in my face. Her lipstick is bright red, and smeared a little on her bottom lip. "You caught me!"

"Yeah, all right—" I say, trying to get her to stand up. "Seriously, Jenna…"

I see her brown eyes flick down to my mouth. I realize half a second before she kisses me what she's about to do. Her face zooms toward mine, her eyes half-closed.

"Jenna, what the fuck are you doing?" I ask, genuinely perplexed.

I manage to grab her by the shoulders and hold her back, but that just makes her laugh deliriously.

"You think I haven't seen you looking?" she says. "I know you've been watching me. You all have."

"What? I—"

She grabs my dick through my jeans, which makes me reflexively crumple inward. "Get the fuck off of me!"

Then she goes in for the kill while I'm completely off balance. She kisses me, groaning obscenely.

Which is the perfect moment for Asher to walk in.

"What the fuck?" he says, aghast. "Jenna? Jameson? What the fuck!"

I manage to push Jenna off, wiping at my mouth. I turn to Asher. "She jumped me."

Wham! I almost don't see his punch coming. He put his whole body into it, though. Asher's almost my height, and bulkier than I am. His punch lands on my lower lip, which is more surprising than anything.

It knocks me back a few steps. I'm stunned. I feel a trickle of blood seep out of my mouth. "What the fuck?" I ask, touching my lip.

"You fucking prick!" he screams.

"I'm not the one you should be yelling at, dude!" I point to Jenna, who has started laughing uncontrollably.

"You're both such pieces of shit!" she declares. "Fuck you both."

Asher flushes a deep red. He wasn't expecting that, I guess. He turns and storms out of the back room.

I'm right on his heels. He lets out a bellow as he reaches the bar, and he sweeps a tray of champagne flutes off the bar top to the floor. The whole party comes to a halt, though the music continues.

"This wedding is off!" Asher yells, making a beeline for the front door.

"Asher—" I try, but he pushes open the door and disappears.

I take a breath, and realize that every single person in the bar is staring right at me. Not to be outdone, Jenna stumbles out of the back room and promptly throws up everywhere. Her dress is split down the back and barely covering the essentials, which only makes her seem more pathetic.

She's noisy, too. I look back at her, feeling absolutely nothing. No hatred, no anger really... just an emotional vacuum.

Well, at least the would-be wedding guests aren't staring at *me* anymore.

Several people rush toward Jenna, and I'm more than happy to get out of the way. Forest comes over to me, looking pissed.

"What the fuck?" he says. "Jesus, you're bleeding."

"Jenna came into the back room and came on to me," I say, loudly enough that a couple of the people helping Jenna turn their heads and glare at me. "Asher just happened to come in at the wrong moment."

"Come on," Forest says, tugging me out from behind the bar. "Let's get your face cleaned up, man."

He hauls me to the bathroom, intent on getting the blood off of my face. When we come out, the bar has emptied out. That's a relief of sorts.

I sit at the bar, while Forest heads off to find his fiancee. Gunnar and Maia are stacking champagne flutes on the bar, looking gloomy. I put my head down on the bar, feeling the coolness of the slate countertop.

I didn't actually *do* anything, but I feel like I fucked up Asher's wedding somehow. I bet Asher feels that way, for sure.

I hear a clink, and lift my head to find Emma on the other side of the bar, setting a bottle of Bulleit bourbon next to my head. She has two oversized brandy snifter glasses held in one hand as she walks around the bar and takes a seat beside me.

I try not to notice her curves, but there is absolutely no denying that they're there in that sexy as hell dress of hers. And her eyes look amazing right now, like two perfect emeralds.

Stop, I tell myself. *You're being a creepy old man.*

"I feel like you need this," she says, tilting her head to the side. She sets down the brandy snifters and uncaps the bourbon, pouring a little for her and a lot for me.

I grimace. "Yeah, I probably do."

I take the glass that she holds out, then clink my glass to hers.

"Cheers," Emma says. We both take a sip at the same time. I sigh as the liquid fire burns its way down my throat. Emma swallows and makes a face.

"Gross," she says, shuddering. "How do you drink this stuff?"

I make eye contact with her as I tip my glass back, emptying it in a few swallows. She smirks and shakes her head.

"I assume you're going to tell me what happened with Jenna?" she asks.

I look at her. I can feel her eyes on me, giving me an appraising once-over. What does she see? A thirty something man that does nothing but bartend and surf? The oldest son of two addicts, who abandoned their kids and left me in charge at fourteen?

There's nothing good for her to see, that's for sure.

Much as I'd like to know just what she's thinking, I resist. Instead, I reach for the bottle of bourbon.

"I'm gonna need way more of this. Then maybe I'll tell you." I can't help the glance that I shoot her, the flirty one. "If you're good."

Emma's cheeks darken prettily. I pour myself some more whiskey, ignoring the voice in the back of my head that's saying that this is a bad idea.

I hold my glass aloft. "Bottoms up."

5

EMMA

I roll over in my bed, frowning when I hit something hard and pointy. My eyes open a crack, and I see shirtless Jameson mere inches from my face. I ran into his elbow, apparently.

Oh, shit.

My mouth goes dry as I take him in. His rakish dark hair, his broad brow and proud nose. His eyes are closed, but I take the time to appreciate his dark eyelashes, resting on his cheeks. And his cheekbones... I never knew that men had cheekbones that were so... enviable. Even covered in stubble, they are friggin *dreamy.*

Then I noticed them on Jameson, and I haven't been able to un-notice them. I swallow hard. He's just so... *big.* And so...

Unf. I hear that noise in my head every time he gets a heavy box down from a shelf. Just... *unf.*

I look down further, to his strong shoulders, his incredible arms, his muscular pecs and abs. It's almost unfortunate that he has the sheet tucked around his groin. But also not really, because I don't think I could keep my hands to myself right now if he were completely in the nude.

I had a hard enough time last night, when I brought a very drunk Jameson back to my apartment. He was planning to sleep at the bar, not wanting to go back to the house he shares with Asher.

Being the hero that I am, I offered to take him back to my place... for sleep. And I was treated to a rare view of drunk Jameson letting it all hang out. And by that, I mean, his cock jutted proudly toward his stomach as he focused on me.

Then he staggered toward me. I was pinned there, frozen, wondering if all my teenage dreams had come to life. Just standing there, blinking up at him, mouth a little bit agape. He grabbed me by the back of the neck and descended on me, his mouth connecting with mine.

There was no time to think or protest. His lips were hot and wet against mine. I opened my mouth to him, and he took what I offered, sweeping my tongue with his. I closed my eyes, tasting burnt sugar and whiskey on his breath.

He growled with a kind of male satisfaction, and the sound curled my toes. Then he let me go.

"Fuck, I'm drunk," he muttered.

And then he passed out in my bed.

All of it happened right in front of me, because of who I am. I'm Emma Alderisi, Asher's little sister and the golden child of my rich parents. My mother and father did such a good job of raising me to have impossible standards for men and the world in general, that I'm *still* a virgin at twenty four.

My gaze slides to Jameson, and I bite my lip. He doesn't know that part, of course. Just like he doesn't know that since I was age fifteen, I've had a plan.

A plan for Jameson to be my *first*.

Unfortunately, despite all my flirting, Jameson basically doesn't even know that I'm alive. To him, I'm just Asher's innocent little sister.

If only he knew even a hint of what goes on in my head...

Yeah, I know that Jameson is as black as I am white. I know that he never finished high school. I know that until a couple years ago, he was bartending and surfing, not looking for anything more than that.

I know that he's almost a decade older than me. I really, really do.

But those facts don't change how I *feel* about him. If anything, they only increase the tangled knot of emotions I feel every time Jameson so much as glances my way.

Across from me, Jameson stirs. He groans and his whole face crinkles with displeasure before he even opens his gorgeous brown-black eyes.

"Ffffffffuckkkkk," he whispers.

Then he opens his eyes. It takes his a second to look at me, but when he does, his dark eyes go wide. "Holy shit. What the fuck are you doing in my bed?"

I smother a grin. "Look around you. This is clearly *my* bed."

He looks around, and curses again.

"What the hell am I doing here?" Then his panic seems to redouble. "Oh god, we didn't—"

He peeks below the sheet he's wearing, and goes pale. I can't help but giggle.

"No, we didn't do anything." I roll my eyes. "First off, you were way too drunk for that. Like... really, really drunk. And second, you would remember if we had sex."

I add a little smirk to the last statement. The flash of relief on his face is kind of comical. Kind of hurtful, too, but mostly funny. Jameson just groans and pulls a pillow over his face.

"I might still be drunk," he mumbles, muffled by the pillow. "Jesus, if Ash realized that I was here right now, he'd kill me. And if he thought I actually fucked you? He'd burn down the bar, and then our house, and *then* murder me."

I sigh. "Yeah, yeah. I get it. I won't tell Asher where you stayed. You just looked like you needed somewhere to sleep that wasn't Cure."

Jameson pulls the pillow off his face, squinting into the bright sunlight that streams through my bedroom window. "It wouldn't be the first time, and it won't be the last."

"Hmm," I say, noncommittal. "Well, I have to go to the law library. I can leave you here to keep sleeping..."

"Uh uh," he says, heaving himself up. "I have to get moving.

Otherwise I will just stay in your bed forever. You don't want that."

I want to say, *Promise?* But I don't.

"Since you're awake, how about some coffee?" I say. I have to try not to swallow my tongue when he stands up, giving me a nice long look at his muscular ass.

I never thought that I even cared about asses until this exact moment. It's a revelation. I can make out the faint tan lines that he gets from wearing his wetsuit halfway off.

All too soon, he finds his jeans and pulls them up his long legs. No underwear. That's another fact that I won't soon forget.

Of course he doesn't wear underwear. How very *Jameson* of him.

"Coffee would be great," he grouses, turning around. "Have you seen my shirt?"

I point to the lamp, where his shirt landed last night when he was stripping. He turns away to get it.

I stand up, realizing that I'll probably need to put on more than the oversized tee shirt and tiny sleep shorts I'm wearing. Luckily, Jameson asks for the bathroom next.

"Down the hall, to the right," I say. I breathe a little sigh of relief. I want to seduce Jameson, but I don't want to just get *naked* in front of him. That would be weird.

I quickly change into a new bra and panties and a light blue floral dress. By the time Jameson is back, I'm pulling my hair into a messy side braid and slipping my feet into a pair of heels.

"Coffee?" he asks, peeking in the room.

"Go to the kitchen," I say, shooing him. "To the left."

I grab my heavy satchel of books and my phone, then follow him to the kitchen. The kitchen is tiny, with all the appliances half size. Jameson looks hilarious standing in my miniature kitchen, like a giant who has lost his way.

"Sit," I order, pointing at the lone chair. I sling my satchel down, and it hits the floor with a hard thump.

"Jesus, what have you got in there?" he asks, taking the seat.

"Runes, incantations. You know, everything I need to nurture my coven," I say. He smiles at that for a split second, before frowning. I start putting the water on to boil, and getting the French press down from a high cabinet.

The ritual of making coffee feels soothing after my morning of combined lust and nerves. I measure the beans and grind them, then pour them in the French press with boiling water.

My roommate Evie comes into the kitchen, stopping short when she sees Jameson. Evie is a gorgeous coffee-skinned trust fund kid that sometimes picks up shifts at Cure. She is still wearing the same teal cocktail dress that I saw her wearing last night, and her hair is a total mess.

"Uhhh…" she says, looking between Jameson and I.

"Hey Evie," I greet her casually. I'm clearly ignoring the fact that it's a little weird that Jameson is here… and the fact that Evie has clearly been out all night. "I'm just making Jameson some coffee. Want some?"

I pour a cup, handing it to Jameson. The scent is lovely, filling the tiny room we're in. Evie seems a little slow to process my words. She shakes her head, her gaze still shifting between me and Jameson.

"Nah," she says, wrinkling her nose slightly. "I'm um… gonna go to bed."

"Okay," I say, giving her a slightly concerned look. "You doing all right?"

Evie turns bright pink. "Yeah. Just… I'll talk to you later. And Jameson, I'll see you later this week."

"Sure," he mumbles, unconcerned with anything except his coffee cup. He manages to drain most of it, despite the fact that I didn't offer him milk or sugar yet.

Evie slips out of the kitchen. I pour myself a cup of coffee. Even as I inhale the scent gratefully, Jameson stands up and sets his cup in the sink.

"I should go," he says. "Thanks for… you know."

"I think of myself as your savior," I say, teasing. "Without me, you'd be waking up with allllll kinds of body aches right now."

One corner of Jameson's mouth lifts. "If only you could do something about Asher."

"That's too much to ask, even of me." I'm joking, but only partially.

He shakes his head, looking down. Brooding, as always. He's so damn good looking, it's kind of hard to watch him.

"I'll see you later," he says. And then he's off, finding his own way out of my apartment.

I sip my coffee, burning my mouth a little. The bitter taste makes me pull a face, and I set my coffee on the kitchen counter. I'm pulling a gallon of milk out of the fridge when Evie comes back.

She's changed out of the teal dress, but her hair is still a complete bird's nest. I glance at her.

"Change your mind about coffee?" I ask.

"Nope," she says, shaking her head. "I heard him leave. Now I want the scoop! What the hell happened?"

I *might* have gotten drunk and confessed my love for Jameson a few times since we've lived together.

"With Jameson?" I ask. I sigh dramatically. "Nothing. He was drunk. He couldn't go home. I saved him from a night of sleeping in one of the booths at the bar, that's all."

She arched her brows, the very picture of disbelief. That face of coy skepticism is how I know that she was born with money. My mother and her friends used to do it all the time.

"That's it?" Evie says.

"That's it," I say. I hold up my right hand, with two fingers pointed up. "Scout's honor."

"Mmmhmm." She doesn't look altogether convinced. Evie opens the refrigerator and pulls out a bag of baby carrots.

"Should I even ask where you've been?"

She blushes. "Me? I haven't really been anywhere."

"That's not what your sex hair is saying to me right now," I say, gesturing to the hair she's unsuccessfully attempted to pin up.

Evie munches on a carrot. "I take the fifth on that one. Anyway, I have to go crash. I desperately need sleep."

"Mmhmmm," I say to her retreating back. She waves a carrot in the air as she disappears out of the kitchen.

I check the time on my cell phone, and then hurriedly gulp down my coffee. I have a Constitutional Law study group soon.

I rush to the law library ten blocks from my house, but I find that it's impossible to concentrate. I blame the material, honestly.

Why study about what John Locke said about the law when I could focus on much more fascinating things? Like Jameson's full frontal nudity in my bedroom last night.

I may not know a ton about penises, but his was... definitely intriguing, to say the least. Long and thick, but also delicately pink.

Like the man himself, I wouldn't even know what to do with it if I get my hands on it. That didn't stop me from daydreaming about it though, did it?

The day goes by fairly quickly in that manner, and before I know it it's the afternoon. When I am finally done not-really-studying at the law library, I pack up my books and head to Cure.

I get there just as Jameson is unlocking the doors. He looks as mouthwatering as ever, wearing a deep navy v-neck, a dark pair of jeans, and his black Converse. He's also carrying a black back pack, which gives me pause. I don't think I've seen him with one since we were kids.

Even though I saw him literally hours ago, I salivate a little bit and my pulse speeds up. He turns and sees me as he's shouldering the door open.

"Hey," he says. I shiver and blush as I feel his eyes on my chest, my bare legs. "Long time no see."

"Ha," I say. I wish I had something more, but I don't.

To my surprise, he holds the door open for me. I step inside into the darkened bar, brushing past him.

"Help me get the blinds open, will you?"

Jameson is all business right now, his mind obviously making a list of things that need doing. I'm not an actual owner per se, but being Asher's sister, I get free drinks and food in exchange for occasional help.

I set my heavy satchel on the bar, then get busy opening the blinds, letting the afternoon sunlight pour in. Jameson disappears into the back, probably counting money or something. When I'm done, I go to the iPad they use as a register and put some Sade on the stereo.

As the sultry music begins to fill the bar, I plop myself down at the bar. Jameson's backpack is right there, and it's open a little. Biting my lip, I look up and make sure that he isn't about to come back.

Then I hook a finger on the gaping zipper, glancing inside. On top of everything else, there is a book. The last book I would ever expect Jameson to be carrying around, honestly.

It's a GED Math textbook. I push it aside with a finger, and see that he's also carrying around science and social studies.

I know that Jameson quit school young. When his grandmother died, he left the ninth grade to work and take care of his younger brothers. I didn't realize that he even cared about not having a diploma, or that he was studying for the GED.

"Hey, do you—"

I look up, startled and guilty, as Jameson comes out of the back room. I snatch my hand back, but it's too late to be subtle all the sudden. He sees what I'm looking at and turns a little red.

Oh my god, this might be the first time I've ever seen him blush. I didn't even know that embarrassment was even possible for him until now. He's always so self-assured and confident.

Cocky, at times. To find out that my perception of him is skewed... it's a jolt.

"Sorry!" I blurt out. "I'm just... nosy. And curious."

He comes over the the bar and grabs his backpack. "It's nothing. Just something I'm thinking about."

"It's not nothing," I say.

Instantly, I know I've said the wrong thing, because his expression grows guarded.

"Not everyone has a rich family that can put them through law school," Jameson growls, heading toward the back room.

"Oh, Jameson—" I say, but he vanishes from sight. I push myself to my feet, hurrying around the bar. When I get into the office, I find him counting the drawer for the cash register.

I wait until he is done, leaning up against the wall. He keeps glancing at me, aware of my presence, but he doesn't stop what he's doing.

When he's counted the last bill, I take a deep breath.

"That came out wrong," I say. "What I meant was, I think that if you're interested in taking the GED, you should."

"Thanks for your permission," he says flatly. But at least he's not growling at me anymore. He moves past me, back out front, and I follow.

"I just never realized you were interested in it. Honestly, between surfing and working here, I kind of figured you had moved on."

Jameson doesn't respond. I'm worried that I'm digging myself deeper and deeper into a hole. What can I say that will make this better? He starts pulling fruit out of the lowboy coolers, lemons and limes and oranges.

"Hey," I say, drawing at straws. "How much do you know about algebra?"

He glances up at me, grabbing a cutting board. "Not a whole lot, as you can imagine."

"But I bet you know basically everything about surfing, right?"

He digs a blade out from somewhere behind the bar and begins slicing lemon and lime wedges. "I like to think so."

"How about a trade, then? I tutor you for the GED, because I have a crapload of extra knowledge. And you tutor me in surfing, because I've never even touched a board."

He paused, his knife in the air. "Never?"

"Not even once. Mother said it was unseemly." I roll my eyes.

"I don't know," he says, frowning. He goes back to cutting lemons and limes. "I don't think Asher would like it."

"Come on. Asher's not even talking to you!" I cross my arms. "And I'm serious! I want to learn how to surf."

And maybe spend a little more time with you, in less clothing, I think.

He just gives his head a tiny shake. "Unh uh."

"What's the slope of a line?" I ask. "What is the quadratic formula? Or the Pythagorean theorem?"

The tips of his ears grow red. "I don't know."

"That's why this is perfect!" I declare. "Seriously, you could probably be ready in like a month. And I could use the vitamin D from being on the beach. It's good for mood elevation. It will be good for both of us!"

I hold my breath, waiting. Jameson hesitates.

"Your brother can't know about it," he says. "He already thinks I'm a fuck up. Even without ruining his wedding, which he definitely thinks I did."

I can't contain my grin. "Yes! You will not regret this. I promise."

As if summoned, Asher pulled the door open just then. He doesn't have the I've-just-eaten-a-lemon expression that I expect him to, but he doesn't look happy either.

I'm just shocked to see him so soon, honestly. I figured he would hide out for a week or so, lick his wounds.

"What?" he barks at me. "Find somewhere else to study. It's Saturday. We're going to be busy tonight."

He storms past Jameson, not even making eye contact with him. I look to Jameson, but he just nods gently.

"He's right," Jameson says.

I roll my eyes, then hold up my phone. I mouth I'll text you.

He glances toward the back, where Asher disappeared. He doesn't say anything else, so I grab my satchel and head for the door.

I walk the block to the beach, shading my eyes against the brightness of the afternoon sun. The ocean is there, waves crashing on the beach. I am going to teach Jameson. And he's going to teach me.

Hopefully, if I have anything to say about it, he'll be tutoring me in a lot more than how to catch a wave. Smiling to myself, I wander down the beach.

6

JAMESON

The next day at work, I'm relieved that I'm not scheduled to work with Asher. Instead, it's me and Gunnar opening, with Alice and Maia showing up a little later.

I go about my bar prep silently, thinking about what a shit show last night was. It was busy as fuck, and Asher was pretending I didn't exist. To say that last night was rough was an understatement.

I wish I could rage about how fucked up it was, and how I didn't see any of it coming. But the problem was, I kind of did.

I love Asher. Straight out, flat out love him. He's as much a brother as Forest or Gunnar. I'd stick with him through hell, if that's what's needed. When we got drunk at his engagement party and he said he had a plan for Cure, I was with him even though he had no idea what he was talking about.

The problem is his fiancee. Or ex-fiancee, I guess. Jenna has always been weirdly jealous of Asher's time. She resents any time he has to spend at Cure, throws a fit once a week.

Then there is the fact that she treats everybody like dirt. Only that's not even the *bad* part. Most of all, the way she refers to the future is what makes me hate her.

She's always so sure that he's going to tire of the bar, that eventually he will grow up and suddenly like her friends more than us. She's made herself perfectly clear on this topic a number of times.

That's why I was so thrown yesterday when she made her move, trying to grab my cock and trying to kiss me. It just seemed to come from nowhere, but maybe that's just some rich person shit that I can't even understand.

The part where it became my problem is the part where I decided to confront Asher. Rather than hear what I was saying and take it under advisement, he freaked out. Then he lashed out.

Things have been strained for a good couple of months now, but I didn't expect anything like what happened the night before last. Asher walking in on that, and assuming that I did something wrong...

It was pretty brutal.

As customers start to filter in I run the service well, not inclined to stand and talk to customers. I like working the service well on days like today, because I don't really have time to think.

Maia and Alice ring in the tickets, and I have to make the drinks. Most of the cocktails I know from memory. It's sort of like an assembly line, slight variations on the same six or seven drinks.

I do it for almost four hours, filling the time in between orders by running the undercounter dishwasher and restocking liquor up on the shelves.

It's not until Gunnar comes up behind me, clapping me on both shoulders, that I pause to look around. The bar is quiet, which is pretty normal for a Sunday night.

"You can get out of here," he says. "I'm about to send one of the girls home too. I know you guys were slammed last night. You probably didn't get much sleep, huh?"

"I mean, I'm fine." Even as I say it, though, I feel the pull of wanting to leave. "Actually... yeah. I do want to get out of here early."

"I knew it," Gunnar says. "I'm psychic."

"You sure you're good?" I ask, rubbing the back of my head.

"Yeah," Gunnar says good-humoredly. "I got this."

I clap him on the shoulder and head to the back room. I switch out my bartender's apron for my hoodie, grab my backpack, and then hit the front door.

It's officially dark by now. I walk to the beach, which is just a block away. Even though I can't see much of the ocean, the salt spray and the sound of the waves work their magic. I take a deep, calming breath.

I walk a little ways down the beach, my thoughts scattered. I feel my phone buzz in my pocket, the first time I've felt it all night.

I pull it out and realize I've missed a few texts from Emma.

Hey! What are you up to?

Wanna study?

About to get in my pajamas if you don't text me...

The last one is only a minute old. I see an image in my head of her in her pajamas, which is burned into my brain from earlier this week.

I know I need to get my mind out of the gutter, but I can't help it. I smile a little to myself as I text her.

I'm here. Just left work. It's not too late to study, is it?

A few seconds later, I have my reply.

Nope. Wanna come over here?

I really, really do. But I just text back: *Sure. Be there in 5.*

I walk to her house, just a handful of blocks from the beach. It's a ramshackle little house painted baby blue, and barely big enough for two bedrooms. No yard to speak of, just sand surrounded by a white picket fence.

When I approach the house, Emma is sitting on the porch, reading from a huge textbook. Her dark hair is braided around her crown, her long legs looking sunkissed in her little short shorts. She's wearing an oversized pink shirt and no shoes, and she's curled up comfortably on a big gray papasan chair.

This is really a terrible idea, a voice says in the back of my head. Just one glance at her, and I am already feeling guilty as fuck. But I shove the voice away and let myself in the squeaky white picket fence's gate.

Emma looks up and smiles, her blue eyes warm.

"Hey," she greets me.

"Am I interrupting something?" I ask, nodding to her textbook.

She shuts it, shaking her head. "Not at all. I was looking for any reason whatsoever not to study property law."

"Mmm," I say. I look at the empty chair beside hers, stacked with a couple more textbooks. "Can I sit down?"

"Yep." She pulls everything off of the chair and stacks it neatly on the floor. "Make yourself comfortable. Do you want something to drink?"

I sit down, suddenly a little self conscious. The chair is a plain wooden one, and it's too small for my big frame. I take my backpack off of my shoulder, putting it on the floor. "Uh... nah."

"I have wine," she says, her expression thoughtful. "A couple bottles that Asher brought over here. Pinot noirs, I think."

"No thanks. I'm still trying to completely get over Friday night's drinking binge," I say, pulling a face. "You can drink if you want to, though."

She waves a hand. "Not necessary. Did you bring your books?"

"Yep." I unzip my backpack and pull out the science and math GED prep books. "I'm not even sure where to start."

"Do you have a studying plan? Certain days of the week, you study certain subjects? Or..."

My lost expression is enough to stop her words. I shake my head, out of my depth in this arena. It's not a comfortable feeling.

"Okay," she says. "That's not a big deal. I think it would be best if we set up a studying system, though."

I incline my head. "If you think so."

Emma smiles at me. "I think so. Let's see... how many days do you have available to study, for how long?"

She reaches out and grabs the math book from me, her hand brushing mine. I swallow, trying to remind myself that I'm not a middle schooler, and this isn't a soap opera. There is no hot-for-tutor thing going on here.

I shift in my seat, willing my body to comply with my brain's wishes.

"Probably two nights a week, one or two hours?" I answer.

She looks up from my book, biting her lip. "Is there any way you can do three days? And make it two hours? That would really be ideal."

I hesitate, then shake my head. "I don't think so. At least on the number of days. I've got Cure to run, and I have to surf at least a couple times a week. Otherwise I'll lose my shit on someone, real quick."

She looks a little nonplussed, but she shrugs.

"Okay. Probably then like... a month and a half, or two months," she says, flipping through the book. "I hope you can cram a ton of stuff in your brain."

"Well, it helps that it's broken down by section. I've already taken the English and social studies parts."

Emma lights up. "Really? You did?"

I nod.

"I can't believe you didn't tell anyone!" she says, punching me lightly on the arm. She wrinkles her nose. "Jesus, it's like hitting a rock or something."

I chuckle at that. "Do you need me to flex for you?"

She grins. "Maybe later. Where are you in this book?"

I shrug, growing uncomfortable again. "Mmm, about a quarter of the way through it. I'm not feeling sure about any of it though, honestly."

She purses her lips, thinking.

"Alright. Let's start by taking the first practice test in the book. Then I can see where you're at, and go from there."

"Okay." I move a little closer to her, to see the book.

She smiles at me, tucking a wisp of hair back behind her ear. When she looks back down at the math book in her lap, I notice the slender column of her pale neck, dotted here and there with tiny freckles.

She flips through the book and locates the first test. "Here we go. You ready?"

I nod. Emma asks me the first couple of questions. They're

simple enough, with the math in them easy to do. Then I have to pull out a notebook and pencil for the next few questions.

"It looks like you've got most of these down, no problem," she says when I've finished the test.

"Yeah. It's more like... the formula you were talking about yesterday. Or that thing that tells you when to multiply and subtract... what's it called?"

"The order of operations?" She waves a hand. "Things like that are easy enough. Really just a matter of memorizing stuff. I can do some flash cards for you the next time we meet."

"Good enough," I say with another shrug. "Now the science stuff... that's a different thing. It's not as easy to work out as math. Math is like... concrete, I guess."

She wrinkles her forehead. "Are you trying to tell me that you're not going to be an astrophysicist?"

"Not anytime soon." I look down, realizing that I'm clenching and unclenching my fists out of pure nervous discomfort. Emma is so fucking educated, and I can barely get the math for dummies stuff she's trying to help me with.

I'm so fucking out of my depths here, it's not even funny. Luckily, she doesn't notice that I'm so uncomfortable... or at least she doesn't say anything.

"Alright, let me look through the science book." She holds out a hand, and I plop the heavy textbook in it. "Jesus. Apparently you have to know a ton of science to graduate high school."

I nod quietly, and she flips through the textbook. "Oh, this is great. It seems like you have more leeway here. Like you can probably guess every other question using reading and logic. That's no sweat for you, probably."

I shrug. "If you say so. I haven't really studied much of the science stuff, because it looks impossible. "

Emma looks up at me, her brow puckering. "Jameson, you're one of the smartest people I know. Seriously, that's why it sort of blew my mind that you were going to even take the GED. When you're ready, this test is going to be your bitch."

I feel my ears grow a little warm. The fact that I'm being encouraged by someone ten years my senior, for something that is so basic… it's a little bit of an ego killer. "I'm definitely going to flunk it the first time, hard."

"No way," she says, shaking her head. "That's the whole point of us studying together. When we're done, you will ace the tests. First time's the charm."

I roll my eyes. "You seem pretty sure of the outcome."

She looks thoughtful. "You need some kind of encouragement. Something big, when you take the test. A reward for your diligence."

"Like what?" I say, giving her a skeptical glance.

"Hmm. I don't know. I'll have to think about it. Do you have any big purchases planned this year?"

"Not really. I have several surf boards. I have a car. I have my bike. I have the bar. Really the only things I want, I have already." And it's mostly true. I do have almost everything I want.

Well, except for a girlfriend, but that's complicated. I broke up with my last girlfriend a few months ago. Between Cure and the GED, I haven't thought about dating since then.

Not that I would say any of that to Emma. I clear my throat, shifting a little to put an extra inch between us.

"Well, think about it. This has been an information-gathering session, more than anything. It will help me formulate a plan of attack."

"Just… don't set the bar too high." I rub the back of my neck. "Remember, I'll probably fail. I dropped out of ninth grade for a reason."

Emma looks immediately scornful.

"Yeah, you dropped out to make sure that Forest and Gunnar had someplace to live. I just—" She pauses, then puts her hand on my knee. It feels warm through my jeans. "I hope you realize that leaving school early doesn't make you dumb."

I get fidgety, hearing her say those things, and stand up. I know it's rude, but it's better this way. "Yeah, all right. Are we done here for tonight?"

If she's surprised by my reaction, I can't tell.

"Yes. Of course." She stacks my textbooks, handing them to

me. I grab them, picking up my book bag and stuffing them inside. "Hey, when are you going to start teaching me to surf?"

I shrug. "Whenever you want. Not tomorrow, but maybe… the next day?"

Her sunny smile returns. "I would like that!"

"I'll text you." I shoulder my back pack, ready to go. I pause. "And Emma? Thanks."

She blushes. "No problem. Next time we meet to study, I'll be more prepared. I'll get a set of flash cards, I think."

Fuck, she is really taking this shit seriously. This is probably not going to end how she thinks it's going to end.

I just incline my head and head off the porch, through her sandy lawn. I glance back once, and see her watching me, those bright blue eyes taking everything in.

This was not a good idea, I think as I head home.

7

EMMA

I glance at my phone for probably about the five thousandth time, though I don't really expect anything new to come across the screen. Everything exciting has already happened. I got a much anticipated text from Jameson, roughing out the details of this afternoon.

Surf lessons today?
Totally! Where and when?

Then there is a lapse, with just those three dots, indicating that he's texting. I friggin' hate those dots. Then, he finally texts me back.

Meet at Joe's Surf? Let's shoot for 2.
Definitely! I immediately text back.

That was at noon. Now it's one fifteen, and I am squeezing into my teeniest tiniest bikini. I look in the mirror in my messy bedroom, scoping out the pale pink triangle top against my suntanned skin.

I turn and check out my ass, indecisive. I glance at the pile of other swimsuits I own, sucking my bottom lip in between my teeth. I might be wearing the smallest one, but it's kind of impractical for anything other than sunbathing. One wave gone awry, and the top will be nothing but a memory.

I heave a sigh just as Evie knocks on the open doorway of my bedroom. She is dressed up like she's going to work, in a little black dress and heels. Her coffee creamer skin is all but glowing, and her dark hair is medium length, done in natural waves. She looks like a million bucks, which is good since knowing Evie her dress and shoes probably cost as much as a car.

She gives me a once over. "Who are you planning to seduce? Is it Jameson?"

I wince. "Is it that obvious?"

"Yeah. I mean, if that bathing suit top were any smaller, it would cease to exist." She looks faintly amused. "He is really ridiculously hot though."

I collapse onto my bed. "I know. But Asher has declared me off limits to him, for whatever reason. I'm like... who cares though, really?"

Evie scrunches her nose. "Are you really into Jameson? I thought you just thought he was hot."

"I do," I reassure her. "I would just like the option to bang Jameson, if that's what I want to do."

"So wear a slightly more normal bikini to the beach with him then," Evie says. Then she frowns, putting her hand in front of her mouth. "Man, I must've eaten something that didn't agree with my stomach."

"Are you okay?" I ask, sitting up.

"Yeah. I'm just nauseated. Anyway, I have to get going. I have to take my car in to the shop." She smiles at me. "Good luck with the seduction, I think?"

I blow out a breath and nod. "Thanks. See you later."

She nods, her mind obviously elsewhere. I poke through the pile of bikinis, and end up with a white bikini with a *hint* more coverage. Then I pull on a pair of flattering denim shorts and a strappy black tank top.

After a minute of dithering, I decide on Converse as my footwear. I grab a gray striped beach tote with my wallet, phone, and sunglasses inside, and head out the door. Jameson is waiting for me outside the weathered looking shop, propped by the front door in his dark jeans and a black t-shirt.

When he sees me, he looks a little irritated. *Uh oh... what did I do?*

"I thought you were going to bail," he says flatly, crossing his arms.

"It's only... 2:10," I say, checking my phone. "You said we were going to shoot for two."

He frowns down at me, squinting into the bright sunlight. "I like people who are punctual."

"Take a chill pill," I say, rolling my eyes.

"You know, maybe this was a bad idea." He pushes himself off the building, moving toward the parking lot. He seems pretty serious.

"Wait!" I say, rushing forward to catch his arm in my hands. His arm feels so muscular under my touch, I almost squeeze it to make sure I'm not crazy. The contact seems to stop him in his tracks. He looks me right in the eyes, his gaze pinning me in place. "I... I'm sorry, okay?"

A long moment stretches between us, with J's expression eventually softening.

"Just be on time from now on," he rumbles.

"Yes. Definitely."

He shakes his head a little, blowing out a breath. Then he carefully steps out of my grasp, clearing his throat. "Let's go inside."

He pushes open the front door, which chimes a little as I walk in. Inside the shop is surprisingly modern, all smooth concrete, polished cedar, and a few chrome garment racks. Along the back wall there are a number of finished boards and three half-finished surf boards. There's also a woman who is sanding one of the boards doggedly.

The song that is playing low in the background ends, and the woman stands up, pulling off a paper respiration mask. She's really pretty, blonde and thin with cutoff shorts and a yellow crop top. She looks at Jameson like he is some dirt on her shoe, though.

"Jameson." She crosses her arms. I'm willing to guess that she has dipped a toe into J's pool, and she didn't like the results.

"Maria," he greets her, ducking his head. "It's been a while."

She gives him a nasty look, then turns to me. "If you're

thinking about dating him, do yourself a favor. Get a nice vibrator, and save yourself a ton of time."

My cheeks turn red. "Oh, we're not—"

"That's not what—" he tries to explain.

I look at Jameson, and he looks at me.

"Whatever," Maria says. "What do you want?"

"We just want to look around," Jameson explains. "She's never even been on a board before."

Maria couldn't roll her eyes any harder if she tried. Her words are huffy and sarcastic. "Great. If you don't mind, then?"

She lifts the respirator mask back into place, turns her back on us, and goes back to sanding.

"Yikes," I say in a low voice. "What did you do to her?"

He just rolls his eyes. "Come on. Come look at their boards."

He goes to the stack of finished surf boards, leaning against each other. He touches the first board gingerly, lifting it almost reverently. It's mint green and a few inches taller than Jameson.

"So there are a million kinds of surfboards," he says, turning it over. "There are longboards and shortboards. The top, where you stand, is the deck. The bottom is usually concave, and has a fin."

He flips the board, showing me the fin.

"Mmmkay," I say, squinting.

"Most boards have leashes, a little cuff that attaches to your leg." He flips the board again, showing me. "The nose of the board can be rounded or inclined, depending."

"What is it made out of?" I ask.

"Polyurethane, usually. Here, there are a few different fin and nose setups in this stack. Here's this... and this one..."

He shows me a few examples.

"They all pretty much look the same," I say with a shrug.

"I'm just telling you so that you have the information. You, of anyone I know, should know the value of that." He looks down his nose at me, which makes me suppress a smile.

"Sure," I agree. I suck my lower lip in my teeth, trying not to look at him as if I want to jump his bones.

Which, at this moment, I really really do.

"All right. Let's look around at the other stuff they have in here." He sets the board down. "Here, check out these wetsuits."

Jameson indicates a rack of wetsuits of practically every shape and size. I wander over, feeling the rubbery texture of a suit between two fingers.

"You'll probably want a wetsuit. It's a personal choice, but the ocean is pretty damn cold." He holds up one that is about my size. "Might wanna try this on."

I grab it. "It's a wetsuit. How bad can the fit really even be?"

He shrugs. "Pretty bad."

I roll my eyes. "Alright. I'll try it on in a minute. What else?"

"Well, then you probably want some surf wax… and some serious sun protection…"

I follow Jameson around the store, trying not to look at the size of his hands and feet, or to check out his ass. I feel like I'm a guy; like I just constantly think about sex when I'm around him.

But only him. No other guy has ever turned my head the way that he does. I sigh to myself as he leads me around the shop.

Will he ever notice me? Will I just be a virgin forever?

I'm not paying much attention as the store tour goes on, and I walk right into him. My face careens toward his, and he reaches out to help me catch my balance. We are really close for a second, our faces only inches apart.

"Oh, sorry!" I say, blushing a bit. My hair scatters all around my face, ever a nuisance.

He steadies me, looking at me for a second. He lifts his hand, brushing a stray strand of hair out of my eyes. "You smell nice. Like… lemons, I think."

He likes how I smell. My breath catches, and I look down at his mouth. *Is he going to kiss me?*

But no. He realizes all too soon that he's too close for his comfort, and makes an effort to stand back.

"Right," he says. "Anyway, I was thinking that you could borrow one of my boards for next week…"

"Next week?" I echo.

He gives me a look. "Yeah, I was saying that we should go out to the beach next week, to test out your skills. I'll bring the sun block and the wax and the boards, you just need to bring a wetsuit."

He looks pointedly at the suit in my arms.

"Right! Yeah. I guess I should try this wetsuit on then."

Jameson looks at his watch. "It's only 2:40... if I hurry, I can catch a few waves before I have to work the night shift at Cure. You don't mind, right?"

I deflate a little bit. I guess it really didn't matter what color bikini I wore today, because he's leaving without seeing it.

"Uh, sure," I say.

"Alright. I'll see you soon, no doubt."

For a second, there's an awkward moment where he stares at me, maybe trying to decide if he should hug me or not. Then he seems to give himself a little shake.

"Later." He turns and strides out of the shop, leaving me there alone.

I make a frustrated sound and turn toward the back, to ask the lady working where I can try the suit on.

8

JAMESON

1 999

"Where are we going, Jameson?" Gunnar asks, squinting up at me. He looks pretty grubby in his oversized green hoodie and too-big jeans. They're hand-me-downs from Asher's closet.

"We're going to Asher's house," I remind him. My voice cracks on the last word, and Gunnar giggles. "He said we should stop by before school."

He's only eleven, and at sixteen I feel impossibly tall next to him. I glance behind me as we walk down 8th Ave, checking to make sure that Forest is still trudging behind me. He's thirteen and about as shut off from the world as he can get; he's got his headphones on, the music turned up as loud as it can go.

I get where Forest's head is at. Normally at thirteen, a kid would be rebelling against a parent or authority figure. But Forest's parents are dead or gone, with the exception of me. I work two full time jobs, making minimum wage at both.

Frankly, I don't have the time or energy to deal with any of Forest's shit.

So Forest has just retreated from the world, preferring to

listen to music or write in his journal. I wish I had that luxury, but that's not my reality. Gunnar tugs on my hand.

"Can we get tacos from the taco stand again tonight?" he asks.

"Maybe," I say, frowning. I do the math really quickly… the rent on our pay-by-the-week studio apartment is due in a couple of days. I can't pay the rent, buy groceries for this week, and still afford to eat out at the cheapest taqueria. I grimace. "Maybe we'll just eat some ravioli out of the can again."

Gunnar doesn't even bat an eye. "Okay."

I thank god that Gunnar doesn't have picky tastes. Grateful for that, I stifle a yawn. I'm burning one of my precious hours of sleep to come out here, because Asher promised *something good*. Beyond that, I am not sure why the fuck I'm here. I yawn.

"Hey, you turned in those papers that I gave you to the new school, right?"

Gunnar wrinkles his nose. "Yeah. The lady asked a lot of questions, but I think she bought it."

I turn to look at Forest, motioning for him to take his headphones off. He rolls his eyes, but takes them off.

"What?" he asks.

"Gunnar said the lady you talked to at your new school had a lot of questions."

Forest rolls his eyes again. "I mean, she asked all kinds of things. But I stuck to the plan, and let her fill in the blanks. I'm pretty sure that she thinks that we're like, illegal immigrants or something."

"Did anyone else ask anything?" I feel paranoid, but this is the third school district that they've been to in as many years. Every time that we draw too much attention, DFACS gets called. Before we know it, Forest and I are busting Gunnar out of a new foster home in the middle of the night.

No way I'm letting that happen again, if I can help it.

"If you talk to anyone for more than a few seconds, I want to hear about it."

He just nods, putting his headphones back on. I slap him.

"I mean it."

"Yeah, all right," he says. Then he purposely turns his music up so loud that I can hear it, tuning me out.

I shake my head a little, hurrying to catch up to Gunnar.

"Everything okay?" I ask.

He gives me a puzzled look, as if to say, why wouldn't everything be okay? I ruffle his hair a little.

We turn right, and the neighborhood suddenly changes. It gets wealthy, with giant houses on amazing lawns. The sidewalks are smoother here, and there are a lot of palm trees everywhere. I don't know how the rich people even manage to keep a lawn alive here, so close to the ocean.

Two women in running gear brush by us, giving us the stink eye. No doubt they are wondering what three kids from the wrong side of the tracks are doing walking here.

"This neighborhood is stupid," I mutter. "Here, let's cross the street. Asher's family lives on the next block."

Owns the next block is closer to the truth. A high fence rises, blocking my view. All I can see is palm trees. We walk past the driveway, where the gate allows us a view of the house. It's definitely fancy as shit, made of light stone, and branching out dramatically.

We keep moving, per Asher's instructions. The fence pops back up, and I walk along it. Eventually we come up on the corner of the fence, where a space is defined between the fence and a cluster of palm trees.

Sitting in the space is Asher, looking comfortable as ever. He looks up from a book that he's been reading. "Hey."

"Hey," I say.

"Hey!" Gunnar shouts. He scowls. "You didn't say Asher was gonna be here."

I give him side eye. "Yeah, I definitely did. Anyway, Asher... what's the big surprise?"

Asher grins, running a hand through his short blonde hair. He stands up, then leads me a few feet away from my brothers.

"You're gonna love this." He digs in his pocket, producing a key. "I have a place for you guys to stay for a few months. It's a hell of a lot nicer than the most recent place you've been in."

I'm immediately suspicious. "Where is it?"

"It's right around the corner, in my guest house. My father is out of town for the next three months, and I don't think my mom has even been out to the guest house since I was a kid. Long story short, I asked if I can set up my band stuff there, and she said yes." He looks extremely pleased with himself.

I am sure that I heard wrong. Life hasn't exactly been rewarding to me.

"I... what?" I ask.

Asher reaches out and claps my on the shoulder. "Dude, I'm telling you that you have a place to stay. Until my father comes back, at the very least. It's a palace, compared to that place you're staying."

For a second, I just blink at him. I'm expecting that he will start laughing and say it's all some sort of joke, even though Asher isn't really like that. I stare him down until he gets uncomfortable.

"Do you want to come check out the bungalow or not?" he asks.

"Are you sure you're serious?" If he is, that would mean that I can spend this month's rent money on food and school supplies. Hell, if we can get a break from some expenses for a little while, I could save enough for a real apartment. My eyes begin to sting

"Dead serious. Come on," Asher says, turning toward the space in-between the fence and the palm trees. "There's a shortcut just through here."

I glance at Gunnar and Forest, then motion for them to follow me. I try not to let the smile show, but I can feel it stretching my face.

We just got ourselves somewhere to stay for a while.

9

JAMESON

urrent Day

I AM deep in thought as I mop the floors of Cure, reflecting on that time that we stayed in Asher's guest house. We were able to string things along for almost a year and a half, sneaking in and out and avoiding the Alderisis.

When Mr. Alderisi eventually caught us and threw us out, I had saved quite a bit of money. I was able to pay for a downpayment on a one bedroom bungalow. I would never have been able to work and watch my brothers and still have a little money left over... not without Asher.

And that is why I have to keep reminding myself that, until the recent stuff with Jenna, Asher's been a remarkable friend. I'm not loyal to many things or people, but Asher...

Asher is good, deep down to his bones. That's why I can't stand to see him with someone who just uses him. And also why I can't betray him, can't sneak around behind his back with Emma.

Not ever.

No matter how tempted I am. No matter my personal feelings.

No matter how amazing she looked yesterday in those ridiculously short shorts. Every time she wasn't looking, I was scoping her out...

But that's all, I tell myself.

It's also why I have gone out of my way to try to apologize to him for the misunderstanding last week. I've waited at home, but he hasn't been there all week. I've tried to talk to him here at the bar, but I've been shut down.

I get that he needs time to pout and lick his wounds, but he's going to have to forgive me eventually... especially since I didn't actually *do* anything wrong.

I check my watch and redouble my efforts on the floors, trying to finish before Alice and Gunnar get here to start their shifts. I finish mopping, then head to the bathroom to stow the mop. I hear the door chime, and assume that one of the other employees has arrived.

When I head back out though, Emma glances up at me from the bar. She's got a stack of books with her, and a notebook.

She also looks fucking hot, in a black miniskirt and a navy striped tank top. I notice that she's wearing lipstick, which is normally not something I'd even see.

What the hell is wrong with me?

"Hey," she says, smiling a little. "I figured this was as good a place as any to study. You don't mind me being here, do you?"

I tamp down any feelings I might be having and shrug. "Doesn't bother me."

Her smile slowly vanishes. "Right."

I head behind the bar, cutting some lemons, limes, and oranges. I keep sneaking peeks at Emma while I work. I can look, I just can't touch. Or even *fantasize* about touching.

Her dark hair is pulled into a messy bun. As she looks down at her textbook, she nibbles on the end of a pen, a little furrow in her brow. Now and then, she pulls the pen from her lips and makes a note of something.

"Do you want something to drink?" I offer, feeling like a creepy old man.

She purses her lips. "Maybe just a water? When I'm done, I'll celebrate with a drink."

I grab her a bottle of water. I try not to stare as she gulps half of it down in one go, her throat moving faintly.

I try not to look, honestly I do. As Gunnar and Alice arrive, I keep myself busy. I work the service bar, making drinks for the tables, and let Gunnar woo his patrons at the bar.

As the bar starts to get a little more crowded, I relax into the rhythm of making drinks and opening beers. I can get pretty zen back behind the bar, not talking to anybody. Just being in my well, my space that I have set up just how I like it.

The drinks are set up for a pretty automatic mixing process. First I pour the liquor in the shaker. Then the fruit juice or liqueurs. Then I top it off with ice, and shake or stir the drink. Finally, I pour it into a glass, usually straining the ice... and top it with a garnish.

The music is loud, some BritPop remix album that Alice put on. I bob my head along to the beat, getting into my groove. I occasionally sip a beer that I keep on ice, but otherwise just keep rolling.

Emma is definitely still sitting at the bar, still sucking on that pen, but I do my best to ignore her.

The rush hits, people streaming in the front door. One of the great things about our location is that there's a boardwalk just across the street. People strolling see Cure, note how busy we are, and they come in droves.

It gets loud, with people yelling to each other and the music just a little louder than that. I dim the lights, setting the mood for the evening. I like it dark and slutty, which is my preferred light setting at most bars.

Eventually, the rush slows, and I can slow down too. I look up to find Emma sliding into a seat opposite where I'm standing behind the bar.

"Hey," she says, smiling a little. Her voice is just the right amount of throaty. "How about that drink? I think I've been a very good girl tonight."

She actually winks at me when she says it, too. I can't help that I immediately get halfway hard; I'm just glad that the heavy leather bartender's apron I'm wearing hides multitudes of sins.

I play it off, as if her words have no effect on me. "What'll you have?"

She twists her dark hair around a finger, sucking on her lower lip. "Mmmm... surprise me. Dealer's choice."

I don't really know what that means, but I remember that she likes drinks with a lot of fruit. I decide to make a Moscow Mule, vodka and ginger beer and lime. I pour it into a copper mug, garnishing the drink with lime.

Then I set it before her. "Here. The dealer felt like making you a Moscow Mule."

Emma's brows lift a little, but she leans in and takes a sip from the straw. "Mmm! That's so good."

"I mean, I do make drinks professionally." I stand back, wiping my hands on a bar towel.

She laughs. "I know. I just meant... I thought that you might serve me something made with whiskey. I was preparing myself for the worst."

I grin. "You've never tried my Lynchburg Lemonade. It's bourbon and lemonade, and even the girliest girl sucks them down like there's no tomorrow."

A moment passes between us, where I realize that what I just said sounds vaguely sexual. She realizes it too, I can tell by her face. For a second, I'm not sure how or if I want her to respond to that.

Then it passes. She makes it easy, rescuing me.

"Would I want to try it?" she asks, wrinkling her nose.

"The next drink I make you will have whiskey in it," I warn her. "It's decided."

She grins. "If you make it, I will try it."

Alice rings in a ticket of wines for a table. I grab it, but Gunnar comes up to me. "I'll take that one. You should get out of here."

I hand the ticket over, cocking a brow. "Do these glasses of wine happen to be for that table of girls in the corner?"

Gunnar smothers a grin and shrugs. "Maybe."

I roll my eyes and start untying my apron. "Have fun with that."

I head into the back room, hanging up the apron and gathering my leather jacket, motorcycle helmet, and cell phone. When I get out to the bar again, Emma is standing in the gaps between the counters, her satchel slung over one shoulder. She looks over at me, looking a little nervous.

"Do you wanna give me a ride?" she asks, tucking a piece of hair behind her ear. Her face heats. "On your motorcycle, I mean. It's kinda late to be walking by myself."

Do I ever, is my first response. But I just cock my head. She's made the walk home alone dozens of times, but I can't say that to her. Asher would never forgive me if anything happened to his precious little sister.

I just need to remember that.

"Yeah, alright," I say, keeping my expression neutral. "It's less than a mile."

She smiles. "Yep. I'm just… really tired?"

She turns her statement into a question, which makes me think that she's full of shit. But I just head out of Cure, expecting her to follow. She's such a flirt, been teasing me all fucking night.

I'll be glad to see the back of her when I'm riding away, I tell myself. But it's not really true, and I know it.

I go around to the back of Cure, where my black Triumph is propped up. Waiting for me.

I start to put my leather jacket on, then pause. One glance at Emma says that I need to offer it to her instead. If we wrecked, she has a lot more skin showing than I do.

"Here," I say, thrusting the jacket at her. It's better to present it as an order, rather than an offer. "Put this on."

She turns pink, but she diligently puts the jacket on. "Thanks."

I open the bike's storage compartment, pulling out the extra helmet I keep for guests. I hand her the helmet, then pull my own helmet on. I climb on first, starting the bike, revving it a couple of times.

I look behind me, to where Emma is standing. She is drowning in the motorcycle jacket, but it looks pretty good on her anyway. You can hardly make out that she's wearing a skirt under the jacket, and for a second I allow myself to picture it.

Emma, butt ass naked, except for my leather jacket?

Fuck yes. My grip on the handlebars gets a little tighter... and I get another half-assed erection.

Great. That's what I get for letting my imagination wander.

"Come on," I say, though I know my voice is muffled by the helmet. "Climb on."

She looks at me with anxious eyes for a minute, then she puts a hand on my shoulder. She swings her leg over the bike, coming into full-body contact with me.

My cock stands at full attention the second we touch. I can feel her soft curves against my hard body. I close my eyes briefly, reminding myself that she's definitely off limits.

After a few deep breaths of the salty air, I reach back and pull her arms around my waist. She immediately leans forward, pressing her tits against my back.

Fuck, I think, gritting my teeth. I have to get her home, that's the only way that this torture ends.

I rev the engine and then pull out. It's after nine p.m., and there's hardly anyone on the road. I play by the rules on the way to her house, keeping it under the speed limit.

A mile has never seemed so long before now.

When I finally get to her house, I pull up out front. She slides off, and starts to pull the helmet off.

Trying not to overthink it too much, I pull out and race away. She can get the helmet back to me some other time.

Right now, I just need a cold shower and some sleep.

10

EMMA

I drum my fingertips on the cool granite table of the coffee shop I'm in, impatient. Jameson is late, even though we just made these plans to study an hour ago. After his speech at Joe's Surf the other day, I don't appreciate it much.

I look down at the textbook I brought, but end up pushing it away across the table. Finals are soon, a fact which is weighing heavily on me. It feels like I'm running out of hours in my day to study. That, or I'm low on actually giving a crap whether I pass my classes or not. I have done everything that I could for a whole semester; now I've just sort of run out of steam.

I honestly wonder for a minute whether I could pass without the finals. Of course, just not taking the final exams is kind of a pipe dream, but it is nice to imagine for a little while.

The door chimes, and I look up to find Jameson entering, looking harried. Even though his expression is close to a grimace, the rest of him still looks good. His dark hair looks windswept, and he is almost edible in his dark jeans and short sleeve black Muse tee shirt, muscles bulging and veins popping. He carries his book bag slung over one shoulder.

He could easily be the rebellious bad boy in any TV show or movie. But if he's the bad boy, what does that make me? The good girl? The ice princess?

I don't like either option. What if I want to play the rebel, just this once?

Jameson looks around, and I raise my hand to get his attention. "Jameson! Over here."

He sees me and heads over, weaving his way through the tables scattered throughout the cafe. "I'm late, and I'm sorry. This asshole in a Mercedes tapped my motorcycle on Longview Ave, and then he insisted on waiting for a cop to show up. My phone died too, so I couldn't call you."

Jameson drags one of the chairs out, slinging his backpack down on the table. For once, I play it cool, surveying him skeptically.

"It's fine," I say, keeping my expression neutral.

He sits down opposite me and gives me a look. "You're mad."

I slide my textbook backward, closing it. "I'm not mad, I'm just thinking of the lecture you gave me a few days ago."

He shakes his head. "I've been punished already, I promise. You should have seen how much of a dick the guy that hit me was. He was really pissed when the cops got there and told him it was his fault."

I roll my eyes. "Okay. Let's just work. What do you have for math today?"

"Formulas, mostly. The quadratic formula, the formula for a line, and… something with bi? Binomics, or something. I very vaguely understand them."

"They're hard," I say with a shrug. "Like pretty much the hardest part of high school math. What have you got for science?"

"Uhhh…" he unzips his back pack and pulls out his science textbook. He flips to a section that is already well-marked. "It looks like today we've got the conservation, transformation, and flow of energy. And also work, motion, and force."

I look at the time on my phone. "Okay. Let's divide the time evenly, half an hour for math, half an hour for science. Then we'll see where we're at, okay?"

Jameson just nods. "Science first?"

"Yup. Let's just go through what the book says…"

For the next hour, we take turns reading aloud from J's textbooks. I stop at various points to explain something, or to sketch a quick drawing of a concept on a blank sheet of paper. For his part, Jameson is nearly mute as I explain, his brow furrowed the whole time.

He does ask for clarification on a few points, taking notes in his notebook. At about an hour, I notice that Jameson is getting anxious and cranky. He's also starting to stare into space.

"Let's call it a day," I suggest, closing his math textbook. "I can see that I've exceeded your time limit for learning."

He sits back, stretching. "Sorry. I just… I guess I've never had to sit still for so long for anything."

I smile, keeping my tone light. "It's not a big deal."

"Well, it kind of is. I mean, you're taking time out of your schedule. So, uh… thanks." He starts to pack up his stuff. "Are you hungry?"

"Me?" I glance at the time. "I could eat."

He looks a little uncomfortable, rubbing the back of his neck with a hand. "There's this pizza place around the block from here that I've been meaning to try. Wanna come? I'll buy, obviously."

I smother a smile. "Jameson, are you asking me out on a date?"

"What?" he says, defensive. "No. Definitely not."

"I just wanted to check. You seemed awfully sincere about the fact that you didn't even think of me that way," I tease. I'm looking for a reaction, and I get one. He jerks to his feet.

"Forget that I asked."

"Wait!" I say, grabbing his forearm. "I was just kidding. Don't be so serious all the time."

His expression is as black as a thundercloud. He carefully disengages from my grasp. "If I'm serious, it's because life makes me that way. Somebody has to be the responsible one around here."

Oooh. I did not expect him to get so prickly about it.

"I'm sorry. I know that you're the big brother. You feel responsible for Forest and Gunnar. I get it."

The look on J's face is skeptical. "I really doubt that, princess."

I don't have a snappy comeback for that one, so I stick my tongue out at him. He pauses, then gives me the ghost of a smile. I assume I'm forgiven.

"Are we going to dinner or what?" I ask.

"Yeah, yeah," he says. "Pack your stuff up."

I grab my bag and shove my books inside. Slinging my satchel over my shoulder, I hurry to follow Jameson.

"Your legs are like twice as long as mine," I complain as I struggle to keep pace with him. He glances at me, flashing half a smile, and deliberately slows his pace.

He leads me around a bland city block, and heads over to a nondescript restaurant. I wouldn't even know that it was, in fact, a restaurant except for the tiny neon sign outside that simply said P I Z Z A. When he pushes the door open, holding it wide for me, I'm not sure what to expect.

But of course it's actually a nice place, with white tablecloths and a scattering of people eating, though it's only early afternoon. There's even an impressive-looking blonde at the hostess stand.

"Hi! Do you guys have reservations?" the hostess chirps.

"We're friends of David Gage's," Jameson says.

The hostess widens her eyes a little. "Of course! Right this way..."

I look at Jameson questioningly as she leads us right to a table by the tiny front window. He just lifts his brows in response. The hostess seats us at a rounded table, puts a couple menus in front of us, and promises that someone will be right with us. Then she scoots off in the direction of the kitchen.

"Who is David Gage?" I whisper.

"He's the chef." Jameson picks up the wine menu, squinting at it.

"The hostess seemed to think that was weird."

"What?" he says, discarding the bar menu in favor of the food menu.

"That you were a friend of the chef." I pick up my menu, studying the salads.

"Oh… David's sort of…" He thinks for a second. "He's never had a thought that he kept to himself. He just says everything he thinks, some kind of radical honesty bullshit. And he's pretty critical. I'm guessing that most of his staff are afraid of him."

I peer at Jameson over my menu. "But you're friends with him?"

"Yeah. The guy's a genius, and a riot too."

A waiter arrives to take our drink orders and tell us the specials. Jameson looks at me.

"Is there anything you don't like on pizza?"

"I'm a vegetarian," I answer. "So… meat."

He folds his menu and looks at the waiter. "Will you ask David to make us a vegetarian pizza? Chef's choice."

"Of course," the waiter says, bobbing his head. "I'll put that in for you."

"And a bottle of whatever wine he recommends to go with it," Jameson says, handing the menu over. "Thanks."

I hand my menu over as well, thanking the waiter. The waiter vanishes, and Jameson and I are alone again.

"So…" I say, trying to think of something to talk about. "Have you talked to Asher at all?"

Jameson frowns. "No, not really. Your brother is a stubborn bastard. Every time I get home, he's not there. And when I see him at work, he's very…"

"Brusque?" I supply.

He squints at me. "I was going to say untalkative. Is that a word?"

I shrug a shoulder. "It gets your point across well enough."

The waiter returns with a wine bottle and two glasses. There is a whole charade that Jameson and the waiter play, where the waiter pours the wine, waiting for him to smell and taste it. The waiter even leaves the cork on the table, which is something I recognize from eating at fine dining places with my parents.

I finally get a little of the wine, which is red. I turn the label toward me, and read it.

"Garnacha. Sounds fancy."

"Mmm," Jameson says, taking a sip. "Your brother would probably appreciate this more than I do."

I taste it, finding it a little more bitter than I expected. I make a face, and Jameson chuckles at my expression.

"That good, huh?" he asks.

"The only wine I've ever had much of is my mother's chardonnay." I sit back with a sigh.

"You tutored me," he says, moving his chair closer to mine. I can't help but feel a little flutter in my stomach at his nearness. "Let me teach you how to taste wine. That way even if you don't like it, you will look fancy when you try it."

I laugh. "Okay…"

"Okay. First you want to take the glass, and hold it by the stem. Apparently that's important so that the heat from your hand doesn't affect the wine."

He shows me how to hold it, and I copy him.

"Okay."

"Next, you want to swirl it clockwise. You get a good view of the color of the wine, and then you stick your nose in the glass." He does, inhaling deeply.

I do the same. "I'm not sure what I'm supposed to smell. It just smells like wine to me."

His mouth kicks up into a half smile. "I'm just smelling the raspberry and cherry notes. Anyway, then we taste… just take a small sip, and kind of roll the wine around in your mouth."

Sipping the wine, I swish it around a little, then swallow.

His mouth quirks up. "You've got a little…"

He reaches out and touches the corner of my mouth with the pad of his thumb. Our eyes meet, and I swallow. I watch his eyes drop down to my mouth.

Maybe he's wondering how I taste right now?

Then he gives himself a visible shake. "Sorry. Um… what did you taste? In the wine, I mean."

"It tastes like wine."

He rolls his eyes a little. "Alright. I taste maybe… black

cherry, cinnamon, black pepper… but overall it's very fruity and full-bodied."

I grin at him. "You sound very proper. A well-mannered young man."

He chuckles. "There's a first time for everything, I guess. And it's a little weird to hear you refer to me as *young man*."

I make an exasperated sound. "I'm not that much younger than you are."

"Ten years," he chides me.

"Almost ten years. We're not that different, you know. It's all in your head." I take a sip of the wine to punctuate my statement.

He sets down his glass, turning serious.

"We couldn't be more different if we tried."

I cock my head. "Do you think so?"

"I do. First off, I basically dropped out of middle school, while you're getting a degree after college."

I give him a hard look. "You dropped out of high school."

"Yeah, but it was in the beginning of the ninth grade year. Anyway, our growing up was… very different. You were always wrapped in bubble wrap, while the world just dragged me over the rocks, again and again."

I couldn't really disagree with that. "I can't help being born rich any more than you could help being born… not rich."

I blush a little. He frowns.

"Right. There are other reasons we don't hang out, though. Like your big brother will beat me to a pulp if he finds out that we had dinner tonight, no joke. And I owe Asher, big time. I wouldn't do anything to mess up our friendship."

"I hate to break it to you, but I think Asher already thinks your friendship is wrecked."

Jameson pulls a face. "Yeah, but I didn't do anything to make that happen. That's my point."

"And yet, here you are, hanging out with me," I say, sipping my wine. "Tasting the forbidden."

He goes a little pink. I'm starting to love that I can make someone so much bigger than me uncomfortable. "I knew this was a bad idea."

"Relax. I'm just teasing you again."

He sighs. "The point's the same. I'm like some wrong side of the tracks nobody, while you're just... you're like a princess who is locked away in her tower of books. You just look down on the rest of us, and pass judgement."

He waves a hand. I feel indignant.

"I am not!" I say, smacking his shoulder. "That isn't fair."

"It doesn't have to be fair," he says, pinning me with his dark chocolate gaze. "It just is how it is."

"What if I don't like how it is?" I say. I lean closer to him. "What if I want to smash the paradigm? What if I want to rebel a little?"

He rolls his eyes. "Yeah... I'm not really in the market for any rebels, just now."

The waiter comes back, loaded down with a freshly made veggie pizza and a couple of plates. He sets them down on the table. "Can I get you anything else right now?"

Jameson looks at me, amused. "Do you have any water for our young rebel over here? She doesn't like wine, apparently."

I flush deep red. "I don't need any. I'm fine."

"I'll bring them just in case," the waiter reassures me with a wink.

That wink makes me want to die.

"Fine," I mumble.

Across the table, Jameson is dishing up the pizza. I take my slice, taking a bite. But I don't taste it, really. As Jameson moves onto talking about a movie that he's seen recently, I'm wondering about his list of differences between us.

Are they really that great?

More importantly, can they be overcome?

I silently sigh, indecisive.

11

JAMESON

I tap my fingers on the dashboard of my Jeep Wrangler, looking at the time. It's 9:55 am, and I'm sitting at a remote nook of Redemption Beach, waiting for Emma. Today is our first real surf lesson, or at least our first one on the beach.

We're supposed to meet at ten. Then again, she might be defiant and show up late, knowing that I can't say anything.

I grit my teeth. Why am I doing this, again?

I look out at the beach in question, which is deserted. With a rocky sand bar located not too far from the shore, this section of beach is often empty. People are afraid that they'll get caught in rip tides and get dragged along those rocks. Fair enough.

But it's totally fine for my purposes, being that we'll hardly get in the water today. I glance at the clock on the dash again, growing tense.

I fidget with my wetsuit, which I'm only wearing on the bottom half of my body. On the top half I'm wearing a t-shirt. It wouldn't normally bother me to be half-naked, but somehow Emma's planned presence makes me extra aware of my clothing choices.

I stare at my clock for another minute, then decide to move. Fuck it, I shouldn't wait around for Emma. I can at least set up without her.

As I climb out of my Jeep though, Emma whips her

enormous Mercedes SUV into the spot next to mine. She's out of the car in a flash, her raven's wing hair tied up, and her shorts revealing a hell of a lot more than they cover.

I take a moment to drink the sight of her in her bikini top and shorts. Her hips and shoulders are super slim, but she has amazing fucking tits and long legs... and an ass that won't fucking quit.

Fuck. Just... fuck.

Emma bounds up to me with a grin. "I'm here on time."

"That you are," I say, doing my best not to look anywhere but her face. That's a sure fire way to get hard, which would be so fucking awkward right now. "Ready to go out to the beach?"

"Yeah. I need to put my wetsuit on somewhere..." she says. She points out a tan tote bag she's carrying on her shoulder.

"You won't really need it today," I say. I force myself to look out at the ocean instead of looking at her.

"Okay. I brought the suntan lotion." She squints at the ocean too.

"Yeah." I grab the two surf boards out of the back of my Jeep. I start to plod out into the sand, not looking forward to her applying sunblock with me standing right there.

I swing the boards up over my head, carrying them by balancing them on my head. The sand underfoot gradually grows more wet and dense as we get closer to the water. Emma trails along behind me, looking around at who knows what. There's not a soul to be seen here on this cloudy day, not even any seals or gulls around as far as the eye can see.

The land vanishes on both sides, falling away to form a small peninsula. There's just the two of us here, alone together. I swallow, realizing that this might not have been the best idea. But it's too late now for that.

When we are a stone's throw from the water, I carefully put the surf boards down onto the sand with a muffled thunk.

I glance over at Emma. "This seems like a good place to settle for the moment."

She scrunches her face up as she puts down her tote bag. "You're the boss."

"First things first. Sunblock?" I ask. "I already have a base layer on, but I could do with another coat on my face."

She nods, producing a tube of expensive-looking lotion from her bag. "Here."

She tosses it to me, and I squirt a little into my hand before tossing it back. I lotion my face as best I can, trying to ignore her as she lotions her legs, her torso, and her chest. She takes special care with her face, but she still leaves a big smudge under her right eye.

But I remember how close we came to kissing when I removed a drop of wine from her mouth at the restaurant a few days ago. There's no way I'm taking that chance again, so I just keep my mouth shut.

"Ready?" I prompt.

"Almost. Would you mind doing my back?" she says, turning away and dangling the tube of lotion over her shoulder. It's kind of an assumption on her part that I'll say yes... but then again, what straight, red blooded man would say no to that?

I grit my teeth. "Alright."

Taking the lotion, I smooth it across her shoulders. I suck in a breath; her skin is sun kissed, incredibly soft, and warm under my hands. I spread it out over her back, admiring the arrangement of tiny freckles I find there. I'd honestly forgotten that she was so much smaller than me, but touching her like this, being so close, I can't help but remember.

"Make sure you get it down low," she says, turning her head to see me. "I don't want a weird lower back sunburn."

I don't say anything, just obey her command. Her lower back is so perfect, with two perfect divots at the base of her spine. Her ass starts just below where my hands are now, so trim that you could bounce a quarter off of it. I lotion her lower back, my hands spreading the lotion out until I am almost gripping her hips.

I won't lie, it's not the first time that I've thought about holding her just like this... and it probably won't be the last. I realize that I am growing hard in my wetsuit, which is a no-go. Releasing her suddenly, I thrust the tube of sunblock at her.

"Done. Take it," I say.

She turns around and takes it, a little smile on her face. I wonder if she waited until she was here to put on the suntan lotion on purpose, just to fuck with my head. After all, she hasn't exactly been discreet about wanting me to notice her.

And notice her I do. All the damn time, even though I'm not supposed to do it.

"Time to get serious," I say, scowling.

"Yes *sir*," she says with a wink. "I like when you're bossy."

I roll my eyes. Picking up one of the surf boards, I move it about five feet from the other, and lay it back down.

"All right. Come stand right here," I say, pointing to the end of the board.

"Okay…" she says, moving.

"The first thing to do is to try to practice your position and body movement here on the beach." I move to the end of the other board. "So we'll get on our knees…"

I kneel, and she does the same.

"Then I'm going to try to hold the sides of the board, maybe two thirds of the way down. Like so." I grab my board so that Emma can see. "Now I pull myself onto the board, holding onto the sides. Keep your hands on the sides of the board, and your arms tucked back. See this weird sort of chicken wing thing that I'm doing with my arms?"

She frowns. "Yeah, sort of."

"Then just push yourself, your head only, up a little." I do the move. "The first few times you surf, you can make it easier on yourself by riding the whole wave that way."

"That doesn't seem that hard," she says.

I chuckle. "We haven't even tried standing up yet. Let's do it from the beginning."

We both return to kneeling at the end of our boards.

"Alright. Grab the sides… yeah, that's right. Pull yourself on. Tuck your arms. Now watch…" I slowly turn one of my legs out so that my ankle touches the board. "I turn my right leg like this. I lift my chest up… then I slowly, carefully slide my left foot forward. I get my balance… and then, voila!"

I open my arms, looking at Emma. Her look of utter incomprehension makes me laugh.

"What the hell did you just do?" she wonders.

"Look, Law School. If I can do it, you can do it. Let's start from the beginning."

We go through the steps ten times, until I'm absolutely sure that she's got it down.

"You got it? Do you feel good about what you've learned so far?" I ask, standing and brushing the sand off my knees.

She mimics me, brushing herself off. She rolls her eyes. "Just because I understand the theory behind something, doesn't mean I will actually be able to do it. It's *hard*."

"You will. Just not today. The water is pretty unsafe here. Instead of a sand bar, it's pretty much just rocks."

She looks pretty skeptical.

"How do I like... spot the right wave? I am guessing I don't just go after the first one I see."

"You're right about that." I scratch my stubbled cheek. "Let's just go out to catch a baby wave."

"I thought you just said the water is dangerous here!" She looks downright distrustful now.

"I mean, for real surfing, it is. But we're barely going out. Not far enough to do any damage." I pick up the neoprene cuff that is attached to my board. "Make sure that you tether yourself to that board."

"Okay..." she says.

She gets her wetsuit out of her tote bag, wiggling out of her shorts and trading them for the suit. I shuck my shirt, but leave my suit where it is. The sun feels good on my bare skin. I'm not sure if it's cheating to use my upper body as a distraction in the face of her nervousness, but I'm going to do it anyway. Still. I can feel her anxious eyes on my back as I pick up my board and head to the sea.

"You're safe," I reassure her. "We're barely going to go in. You'll see."

True to my word, I slog in, floating my board alongside my

body. When I see that the water has risen to her waist, I stop. "I think this will do it."

Emma glances behind her, to where the rocks are. "Are you sure?"

I shrug. "We don't have to ride at all."

She looks indecisive. "Maybe we'll just do it once?"

"That's what I'm talking about." I give her a smile. "Now, for your wave. You want to pick a wave that is coming right at you, not at an angle. Make sure there is plenty of whitewater in the wave, too. Oh! And this is important. When you wipe out, you want to fall behind the board, and wrap your arms around your head. Protects you from the board knocking you in the head."

"Got it, I think." She scans the waves coming. "Not this one…"

"Nope. It's coming in at a definite angle."

She waits, her hand over her eyes, still looking out over the ocean. She looks beautiful like that, the ocean breeze blowing faintly on the dark wisps that have escaped her hair. Her eyes have never looked more green than they do now, here among the waves.

"Oooh!" she says, pointing. "That one?"

"That's great," I say, giving myself a mental shake. "Position yourself…"

I get on my board, lying down, and Emma awkwardly balances herself the same way. I feel the swell of the sea, pulling my board back a few inches.

"Ready…" I call. "Go!"

The wave hits us, and I wait for just a split second, then make sure that she goes first. But she does, so I go too, launching myself toward the shore. Unfortunately, though it is super easy for me, it's not for Emma. A few seconds into her glide, she leans too much to one side. She goes crashing off the side, kicking and screaming, and goes under the water in no time.

"Fuck." I am quick to bail out of the wave too, plunging underwater. When I come back up, wiping at my eyes, she is floundering and spluttering. I swim towards her and reach her in a few short strokes. I grab her around the waist, lifting her.

"What the hell?" she says, shaking her head to clear it of water. She wraps an arm around my neck. "That didn't go as planned."

My lips curl upward. "You surfed, though. For a few seconds at least."

It's only then that I realize exactly how close we are, pressed together by the waves. She looks up into my eyes, droplets of water clinging to her dark lashes. I look down at the spray of freckles across her nose, at her heart shaped lips.

I could do it, I think. I could take her mouth. Explore her taste, dominate her for just a second. I know she wants it just as bad as I do.

If there was ever a moment, it's now.

But then my surfboard bumps against my back, and the moment is gone. A flash of sadness crosses her face, but I ignore it. I'm the one who is responsible here. I'm *always* the one. I take a ragged breath.

"I'm going to put you down," I say. I let her go, and she stands on her own.

"Jameson..." she starts. I don't know what the end of that sentence is, but it can't be anything that's good for me.

I start swimming in. "I think we're done for the day."

She slowly follows me, like a sad little cloud. It starts to weigh on me, as soon as I can stand on solid ground.

I did the right thing, though. I did the best thing for both of us. The only possible thing.

I just have to remind myself of that, from now until... until I'm dead, I guess.

12

EMMA

I'm walking down the sidewalk in my neighborhood, my phone pressed between my ear and my shoulder. It's the early evening, and I have stuff going on. Unfortunately, my parents don't really respect my time, so I'm listening to my mother complain.

"You just wouldn't believe it," Mom says. "I mean, there we are, at the opera of all places, and Karen Vannick had the nerve to show up. Really, I thought when she and Steve divorced, that that would be the last of her. But she was there, dressed like a complete tramp. She had the gall to look at me in my Versace dress and make a snide comment about it! I mean, really!"

"Mmhm," I murmur. That's all that is required for my part in these conversations. I just have to agree occasionally, and my mother keeps up her never-ending stream of complaints.

"Then she asked about how Asher is, knowing perfectly well that he's not a part of our lives anymore. Can you believe it? She asked about that Jenna Kenner, asking about Asher's engagement. Saying that she heard that there was trouble in paradise. It was totally ridiculous."

"Ummm... actually, Asher broke it off. Their wedding was cancelled," I say.

"WHAT?" Mom gasps. "Why? What happened?"

I chew my lip, then opt for the easy out. "I don't know. You'd have to ask your son."

She doesn't care, though. She's already off and running.

"If Asher had just listened to your father and I about going to Yale, this never would have happened."

I roll my eyes. I turn the corner of my friend Cecelia's street, switching the phone to my other ear. "Mom, Asher didn't want to go to Yale. You and Daddy are the ones that threw down an ultimatum about it."

"I just know that Jameson was behind Asher's decision," my mom says. I can actually hear her frowning over the phone. "Your brother always had a soft spot for Jameson, for reasons unknown. Actually, when your father and I found out that he was getting engaged to a woman, we were a tiny bit surprised. I thought that he was mooning over Jameson still."

Not this again. I exhale and suck in a deep breath. My mom always jumps to homophobic bullshit whenever Jameson or Asher is the topic of conversation. I can't get trapped in this fallacy loop again. Trust me, I know that it ends with my mother in tears and me enraged.

"You know what? I am just about to get to the house. I'd probably better let you go so I can get in the shower before I go to bed." A bald-faced lie if I've ever told one, but it's better than being stuck on the phone forever.

My mother sighs. "All right, darling. Don't forget, your father and I are throwing a brunch next weekend. You'll be expected to be there, with bells on. You're the shining star of the family now."

Yeah, but only after you drove Asher away with your ultimatum. I roll my eyes again.

"Uh huh."

"I was thinking you would wear that baby pink Valentino gown..."

"Oh, Evie is trying to ask me something. I'll catch you later!!! Bye, love you!" I say, hanging up.

My mom is definitely infuriating at the best of times, but at least she's less of a control freak than my father. He sees the world as a chess board, himself as the chess master, and all of the people in his life as his pawns.

I have to live with the guilt of taking his money for law school. I'm supposed to be the perfect daughter, the perfect student When I graduate though, I will be free of their expectations.

Or that's what I tell myself, anyway.

When I step into the yard of Cecilia's house party, I am a little wide-eyed. She described it as being a little get together, but clearly it's anything but that. On the porch, people are gathered around someone doing a keg stand. There are tons of people in Cecilia's front yard, staring in twos and threes, laughing and talking.

Rap music pours out of the open front door. I can tell from here that it's packed inside.

I hesitate, and think about going back home. But what's at home? Nothing except for more studying.

I seriously can't study for another second today. So I tug the hem of my short pink linen dress down and make my way up to the porch. I can feel the bass vibrating as I step inside. Cecilia's whole house is crowded with strangers, especially the living room and kitchen. I edge through the party, looking for someone I recognize.

How is it possible that I don't know anyone here? There's a lively dance party going in the living room, and a mysterious red punch being ladled out by some girl in the kitchen. I accept a red plastic solo cup of punch, taking a sip.

It's so sugary-sweet, it makes my teeth hurt. I assume that the sugar is just masking the taste of alcohol, which is okay with me. Glancing around again, I make my way out the back door. It leads down to the back yard, which is every bit as packed as the front yard. Instead of keg stands though, there are some people playing beer pong on one side. The other side has people wolfing down jello shots before they take a running leap onto a trampoline, randomly screaming.

I don't see Cecilia anywhere, which is kind of a bummer. Cecilia's one of my high school friends that I've kept in touch with, enough to know that she has a huge party going on tonight.

"You look like you could use one of these!" a blonde girl says, holding out a bright yellow jello shot. She is clearly drunk, but also clearly happy. She beams at me. I can't not trust her.

"Thanks," I shout. "Cheers!" I take the jello, eating it in quick bites. I try not to chew too much, because the jello shots are made with something kind of noxious. I make a face, crushing the plastic container that the shot was in.

The drunk girl reaches out and pets my hair.

"You're pretty," she says, her cheeks as ruddy as ever. "Like… I wish I was that pretty."

She is *drunk*. "Hey. I'm Emma," I say into her ear.

"Cher," she says with a giggle. "I'm kind of fucked up right now."

"You're fine," I assure her. "You're just drunk."

She beams at me, nodding. I kind of long for her level of not caring. We don't know each other from Adam, but she is petting my hair.

Maybe I should get drunk. I could pass out jello shots at this party. I could be that girl.

"Can I have another shot?" I yell.

"Yeah, good idea!" she shouts. She takes me by the hand and tows me over to a cooler where the jello shots are kept. She dips into the cooler, and comes out with a red one. "Here you go!"

I chew the red one, wincing again at the taste. I don't know what they put in there, but it is almost eclipsed by the sugariness of the jello… almost.

"Come on. Come jump," Cher insists, taking my hand again. She starts to run, and I do too. At the last moment before we fling ourselves onto the trampoline, she lets go of my hand.

Then I'm flying through the air, grinning stupidly. I land just after Cher does, hitting the trampoline's surface. She squeals really loudly, and I let out a little scream as we bounce for a couple of minutes.

Eventually we scramble off the trampoline, to make room for

the next person. I'm out of breath and so is Cher. We take a minute to reassemble ourselves, fixing our hair and laughing.

That's when I look across the back yard and see Gunnar and Jameson emerging from the house. They both look like freaking models, both in head to toe all black. They look so alike for a moment, it's almost as if they are twins.

Like a magnet, J's eyes come straight to me, my hair disheveled and my eyes bright. He looks surprised to see me, like I can't have any fun on my own. That thought makes my smile dim a little.

Gunnar heads over to the beer pong table, and Jameson comes toward me. He's not wearing his leather jacket or carrying his helmet, so he must have come by the ancient Jeep he sometimes drives. Cher giggles, pulling on my arm.

"That superhot guy is coming to talk to you," she says with a grin.

"Yeah, I think so. He's a friend," I tell her, blushing.

She looks at me with wide eyes. "Oh yeah. You're going to get laid tonight."

"It's not really like that—" I protest, but she's already winking and nodding. She turns away, and finds a random guy to talk to instead.

When Jameson reaches me, looking tall and forbidding, he has to lean in close to make himself heard. He accidentally brushes my hair with his hand, the gesture oddly intimate. "What are you doing here?"

His low voice sends goosebumps all over my body. I cock my head, then lean close to his ear.

"Having fun. What are you doing here?"

He looks amused. "Gunnar dragged me here. Of course, he spotted someone right away and left me. I'm glad to see you, because I don't know anybody else at this party."

I smile. "Yeah, I don't really know anyone either. I just had to get out of my house and do something that doesn't involve studying for a while."

He looks around the backyard. "I think I need a drink."

"Oooh! You should have one of the jello shots I just had," I tell him. "They're pretty strong. I already feel a little… fuzzy."

And it's true. Everything does seem to have a slight halo. And it might be my imagination, but I feel warmer, like I'm being wrapped up in a hug by someone much bigger than me.

Jameson makes a face. "I'm going to get a beer. I'll be right back."

I pout for a second, then decide to get another jello shot. I head to the cooler, opening it. Cher appears as if magically summoned.

"Hey, you shouldn't have more than two of those things," she yells. "They are loaded with molly."

I freeze. "What?"

"MDMA, molly. They're special jello shots." She looks pleased with herself for some reason.

"Shit!" I say. "Isn't that like… what people take at raves?"

"Yeah, that's exactly it." She nods along to the music.

"I… I've never taken any drugs!" I protest. "I'm in law school! I don't have time for that kind of thing."

I start to tear up. I am totally out of my depths here. I don't know anything about drugs. Ive barely even smoked pot.

Cher hugs me suddenly. I'm a little bit at a loss for what to do. "Then you need it most of all. Drink a lot of water, okay?"

I see Jameson coming back with a red solo cup, and I pry myself out of Cher's arms. "I think I should leave."

I turn and run to Jameson, feeling panicked. I get close to his ear, cupping my hand to be heard. "Can we leave?"

He looks at me, at the tears in the corner of my eyes. "Yeah, of course."

Without another word, he sets his beer down on the steps. He holds out his hand to me. I take it, feeling lost and anxious. He leads the way through the party, through the house and out to the front.

Once we are a few houses down, the music has faded enough that I can hear him again. He releases my hand, and then I stare at my hand, wondering how it can feel so… empty.

"What's going on?" he asks, gently grabbing me by the shoulder.

I look up at him, noticing again how handsome he is. Strong cheekbones, a prominent nose, perfect brown-black eyes. *Unf.*

"Hey! Say something." He prompts me, shaking me a little. I guess I took too long to answer. I smile, feeling a thousand tiny pinpricks on the back of my skull. If this is the effect of MDMA, I guess it's not too bad...

"Ummm... the jello shots had MDMA in them, I guess," I say. My tongue feels very weird in my mouth all the sudden.

"Whhhat?" he says, perplexed.

"I didn't know," I say. "But I think... I think I'm high?"

"Fuuuuuuck. Do you feel okay?" he says. Jameson leans down, scanning my face critically.

"I think I'm fine?" I say, giggling.

"Okay. We need to get you somewhere. Somewhere that's not public, where you can ride the MDMA out. Do you want to go to my house?"

I frown. "Asher might be there. He can't know."

He sighs. "It's not like you did this on purpose."

"Yeah, but if he comes home and finds me high, he won't let me hang out with you." I reach up, curling my hand into his shirt. "I want to hang out with you, now more than ever. Besides, just thinking about Asher makes me anxious."

He makes a face. "Okay. We can go to your house. But let's set some boundaries, here..."

I jump up and hug him, burying my face against his neck. What I crave right now, what I need, is for him to hug me. Stroke my hair, maybe even kiss me a little.

But he reaches out and forcefully separates our bodies.

"That's what I'm talking about, right there. MDMA makes you reallllly enjoy physical contact. But even though you're high... I think that we should probably limit the touching."

"Why?" I ask. I'm distracted by a neighbor's dog barking. I can't see the dog, but I want to pet it.

Jameson clears his throat. "Unless you'd rather hang out with Asher, just say yes."

I shrug. "Okay. Can we go?"

"Yeah. I'll just text Gunnar later," he says. "Can we walk?"

I grin at him, tilting my head to the side. "Totally. Whatever you say, Mr. Man."

He rolls his eyes. "Great. Let's go."

And with that, the two of us start down the sidewalk.

13

EMMA

As I walk up the steps to my house, arm in arm with Jameson, I can't help but grin. I wouldn't dare say it out loud to him, but anyone who saw us right now would definitely thing that we were going back to my house to screw. Or even more than that, a bystander might assume that we're dating.

I giggle a little at that. The idea of big, bad Jameson showing up to take me on a date is ridiculous.

…isn't it?

"Isn't what, Emma?" he says. I didn't realize I was speaking aloud, and I flush. "Have you got your keys?"

"Don't need them." I fling the front door open. I step inside, grinning like a maniac. "Ta-da!"

He instantly scowls. "Jesus, Em. You two leave your front door unlocked all the time?"

"Yep. Evie lost her key last week. Don't tell any big, scary men, though." I wiggle my eyebrows at him as he closes the door behind himself.

"That's going to have to change," he says. "Not tonight, though. Can we go to your living room?"

"No no no," I say, grabbing his arm and pulling him toward my bedroom. "Come in here. There's an album that I really, really need to listen to right now."

"Can't you listen to it in the living room?" he asks.

I turn a corner and stop dead, making him run into me. "Ohhhh, no. There's no sound system in there."

He rolls his eyes. "Okay."

I continue to pull on his arm, dragging him into my bedroom. Like the rest of the house, my bedroom is tiny. It just fits the bed and a chest of drawers, with an itty bitty closet to match. Jameson has seen my bedroom before obviously, but when we enter the room, he eyes it uncertainly.

"Sit," I command him, pointing at the bed. "I have the album somewhere."

He sits on the side of the bed, looking rigid and uncomfortable. I giggle as I reach for my ipod on the desk, which is hooked up to a bluetooth speaker.

"What's so funny?" he asks.

"Mmm? Oh. I'm just laughing at how you're sitting on my bed like you haven't been naked as the day you were born before in here." I queue up my favorite m83 album, which is appropriate music for the moment, I think.

"Hmm," is his only comment. When I turn around, he is looking at me suspiciously. "I love this album."

"Really? I do too!" I grin, walking around to the other side of the bed. "It's so like… dreamy and atmospheric and intense, all at the same time."

I sit down, peeling my kitten heels off. I sit back on my bed, stretching out and sighing. "This is sooooo nice."

And it's true. I feel great, like thousands of little lightning bugs are just beneath my skin, but in a *good* way. Stretching feels good. Laying still feels good. Everything just feels *good*.

I bite my lower lip. I want to ask Jameson to give me a mini massage, but I don't want him to freak out. Actually, I want to jump his bones, but then he would for sure call Asher to come take care of me.

I would way rather have Jameson as a babysitter than my big brother.

Jameson turns his head to look at me. "Doing okay over there?"

I smile wanly, feeling insanely relaxed. "Sure, I'm okay. I was just wondering how to ask you to rub my shoulders without being weird, that's all."

That makes him chuckle. "Let me grab you a glass of water first. Then we'll talk about shoulder rubs some more."

"Oooookay," I reply in a singsong voice. I hear him get up and leave the room.

I close my eyes, flinging my arms out wide. I feel the bed beneath me, the cotton comforter and sheets super soft, the pillow just firm enough. It's pleasant. The whole world seems so nice right now, capable of sending nothing but good things my way. One of my hands drifts to the short hem on my leg, feeling the difference between the linen of my dress and the smooth skin underneath.

"Here," Jameson says, surprising me by being right beside me. He sits down on the bed, making it creak under his weight, and hands me a huge glass of water. "Drink as much as you can. Your body is running a little warm because of the drugs, and you don't want to get dehydrated."

I take the glass, drinking it down in several lengthy swallows. "Mmm. It's good."

"Want more?"

"Nah, not right now," I say. I set the glass down on the floor, then I sit up. "I want you to rub my shoulders, though."

He looks at me, gauging how serious I am. Or maybe he's trying to tell how high I am, I can't tell.

"I'll be good, I promise," I beg. "I just want to feel touch right now."

Relenting, he sighs. "Okay. Turn around."

He spins his finger. I hurry to do as he says. I really do want to be touched right now, so bad that I have goosebumps breaking out all over my arms, neck, and even my neckline.

His warm hands finally land on my shoulders, rubbing them so intensely that I actually moan out loud. He pauses, lifting his hands off of my skin, but I scoot backward towards him. "Don't stop. Please, don't stop."

Jameson starts to rub my shoulders again, the pressure delightfully hard. I stay quiet, but it's a struggle not to get loud as hell. He works out all the little knots in my shoulders, and then moves to my neck.

Oh. My. God. Has anything ever felt so wonderful? I can't believe that it has.

I close my eyes, listening to the music, which seems to swell and grow. As he massages me, I slowly drift to one side and back, so that I'm pretty much lying down on his lap. But I do it stealthily, so that I'm there before he even notices how close we are.

He tires, and pets my hair instead of massaging me. That's a-okay by me, though. When I think about it, I am living my dream right now. All those teenaged fantasies... all the times that I thought about him while I was using my vibrator... all the moments where I called out his name in this very bed, alone and growing lonelier by the moment?

Yeah, they pale in comparison to having him here with me, in any capacity. Having Jameson in this room is fucking fantastic, and that's a fact.

Eventually I open my eyes, glancing up at him. I look at his short, dark hair, at his gorgeous black-brown eyes, at his strong jawline with two days worth of stubble. I realize with a shock that he's been gazing at me, something dark in his eyes. Lust, longing... or both maybe?

Maybe that's just what I am wishing to be there. But I will him to do that thing he does, for his gaze to drop to my mouth once more.

Then... he looks at my mouth, subconsciously biting his lush lower lip. I can't stop myself from moving my head upward, seeking his lips with my own. He bends slightly, bowing his head. I feel the warmth of his breath fanning across my lips.

He's actually going to do it, I realize.

He closes the distance, touching his lips to mine.

And it's like heaven. His mouth is so much warmer than it ever was in my fantasies, even though this kiss is very light. Exploring, tentative.

I open my mouth a little, letting my tongue find his, stroking it ever so gently. Then he surprises me. He growls, a sound of frustration.

I know that feeling all too well, where Jameson is concerned. So I sit up, push him back into the pillows, and begin anew. This time, we're face to face, our eyes fluttering closed as our mouths open to each other. I put my hands onto the lapels of his leather jacket, clutching them.

I feel his hands on my waist, his touch unbearably light. I feel like he isn't committing to kissing me, and that's just not acceptable. So I nip his lower lip, inviting him to play harder.

After all, that is what I want. I want the whole package, the guts and the glory.

When you look at Jameson, you see this bad boy from the wrong side of the tracks. You can just tell that he likes it rough, that he leaves bruises and bite marks in his wake. You can guess that after a good *long* night, with the right person under his command, he would leave the bedroom with scratch marks and hickies and god knows what else.

War wounds.

So I bite him, just to see what kind of reaction I get. He growls into my mouth, his hand coming up to sink into the hair behind my head. He controls me like a puppet, moving my head just so, giving himself complete access to my mouth. He leans forward, his kiss turning harsher, almost punishing me.

With his free hand, he cups my face, the gesture at once tender and yet still dominant. My breath grows into shallow pants of excitement.

I'm *his*. I'm finally, finally his.

I have never felt anything quite like the way he touches me. I *need* this.

I gasp when he leaves my mouth, gripping my head and turning it to expose the supple column of my neck. I can feel the power he holds back, palpable and obvious. I get goosebumps again as I realize that finally, I am under his thrall.

His hand leaves my face, cupping my breast instead. I moan a little at his touch, arching my back.

More, I need *more*.

Then his kiss slows just before he reaches my collarbone, grinding to a halt. He leans his forehead against mine, his eyes closed, his breath coming in silent gasps.

I open my eyes, and he opens his. I see that combination of lust and longing there again, but this time he pushes me away.

"No," he whispers, his voice hoarse. "No, this isn't right."

He shoves me off of him, standing up. I look up at him, confused and speechless. He shakes his head.

"We can't. Asher would never understand. If he found out, and I lost my best friend..." He looks tortured. "I can't let that happen. Especially not now, when you're high as a fucking kite. Jesus." He takes a couple steps back. "What the fuck is *wrong* with me?"

I find my words. "Nothing is wrong with you. You're attracted to me. I'm attracted to you. It's like... *meant* to be."

Jameson won't hear it, though.

"No," he says, shaking his head again. "This can't happen. This didn't happen, as far as either of us knows."

"But, Jameson—" I start to protest. But it's too late. He's turned to steel.

"I'm going to sit in the kitchen." He starts moving toward my door.

"Wait, let's just talk—"

He looks at me. "This? This... weird thing that's between us, whatever it is? It cannot happen. It can never happen, understand?"

I scowl at him. "But why? Why do you resist something that you so clearly want?"

"Ask your brother. He's the one that makes all the rules in our kingdom."

And then he walks out the bedroom door. Leaving me bewildered, high as hell, and on the verge of tears.

I was so close to getting what I wanted. I could touch him, taste him, smell him.

What will it take to break him? I wonder.

I lie back on the bed, plotting and planning on how I can find out.

14

JAMESON

2004

"Yeah, but... rent is $800. Food is $1200. Car insurance and gas are like... $200, probably..." Forest says, scratching notes on the back of an old flyer. "$200 goes to the bus passes for me and Gunnar. And those are just the mast basic things."

"Man, food is so expensive," I gripe, sitting back.

Forest just nods, lost in thought. I let him do his thing. I suck at math.

We're sitting on the couch that doubles as my bed, trying to figure out how we're going to budget this month. He's only seventeen, grown tall and dark just like me, but he's very serious. Unlike me, Forest is about to graduate high school at the top of his class. He's got a head for numbers, which is why I've asked him for help with this.

"What about Gunnar's class trip?" I ask, leaning over to look at what Forest has written down. "That's another hundred."

He writes that down, scrunching his face. "And what are you going to earn?"

"Depends on the tips. I'll definitely get $400 every week, but tips have been shitty the last month. Maybe... another $50 every shift, six shifts a week." I think about it for a second. "I can go back to working doubles some days, I guess."

"No way. That's how you ended up walking around with pneumonia for two months." Forest shakes his head. "The doctor said you need to sleep like a normal human being. You should let me get a job."

"No," I say, biting off the word. "Your job is to graduate high school. You only have a few more months, and then you're off to California State for a full ride. No ifs, ands, or buts."

He rolls his eyes at me. "So you say."

"I mean it. You're the smart one, dude. One day this is gonna pay off so big. You'll thank me for it then."

Forest gives me a look. "Right, but in the meantime… we're going to be way short."

"So I go back to doubles, then." I don't want to say it out loud, but I was really hoping that wouldn't happen. Working a double shift in a restaurant is actual hell. It's twelve hours of people expecting me to anticipate their every need. "Maybe just two a week. I can do that."

"I mean… that might work…" Forest says. "That's what… two hundred more a week?"

"Yeah, give or take." I sigh. "You're going to have to pick Gunnar up from school again, though. If the school district finds out that we're using an old address, they'll kick you both out."

"He's thirteen. He can take the city bus, just like I do."

I squint. "I don't trust him like I trusted you at that age. He's always showing off, tring to impress girls. I don't think he realizes how serious the school board takes the zoning stuff."

There's a knock at the front door, which always makes me paranoid as fuck. In my experience, it's usually not good news. The door opens though, and it's just Asher.

He's growing out his hair into a long blonde mop, and he's dressed super grungy. It's actually the way I worry that people see me, except he has no reason to be afraid. He's Asher Alderisi after all — super rich, going to Stanford, driving a Mercedes.

His grungy look is just for show. A little part of me is so mad about that… but I shrug it off.

"Hey guys," he says, coming in and closing the door behind him. "What's up?"

"Nothing," I say. But Forest responds at the same time, "Making a budget. We're not sure how we're going to make it this month. You know, the usual."

Forest sprawls back on the couch. I feel the tips of my ears redden. Asher knows that we are strapped for money, but I don't like to talk about it.

"Then it's a good thing I came by," Asher says, scrounging in his pocket. He produces a gift card. "I asked for cash for my birthday, and my great aunt thought that I meant cash for the grocery store, or whatever? I don't know. Anyway, she gave me this gift card, which is like a thousand dollars... but it can only be used at the grocery stores listed on the card."

"Whoa, really?" Forest says, bouncing up to grab the card. "Asher, this is awesome."

I'm not as comfortable with it, though. "Are you sure about that? That's a ton of money."

"Yeah, but I don't like... go to the grocery store. I eat on campus, mostly." Asher comes in and flops down on the folding chair we keep in the living room. "It's not a big deal, honestly. I mean, you'll use it, right?"

"Definitely," Forest says. "Jameson was just complaining that food is so expensive."

I scratch my stubble on my cheek. "Yeah, thanks."

This is how it is with Asher. He gets these amazing things, like this gift certificate, or the second hand beater car that is now parked in my driveway. And then, often as not, he just gives them away to me.

I might need it, but it's still a little uncomfortable. The worst part is that he's not even really aware of the value of what he gives away. I know that if I corner him and wave the stuff he's given me under his nose, he will just shrug.

How do I even begin to start repaying what I owe him? I don't even know how to calculate the cost, honestly.

"Hey, you're off today, right?" Asher asks.

"I am," I say slowly.

"Perfect. I want to go see Hellboy."

"You want what?"

He sighs dramatically. "You work too much, and don't pay enough attention to what's playing at the box office. Trust me, you're gonna love it. You too, Forest, if you're not busy."

"Hell yeah!" Forest says. "Let me get my jacket."

I cast an eye over Asher. He notices me looking.

"What?" he says. "I know you're not going to turn down a free movie and popcorn."

And he's right, I'm not. But I am adding it to the total tally of what I owe Asher, which is growing heavier and heavier the longer we're friends.

15

JAMESON

urrent Day

I KEEP GOING OVER and over the list of what I owe Asher in my head as I go for a run. There are so many things, so many times that he kept me and my brothers from starving or sleeping on the streets. It's an endless litany, really.

But as I get home, exhausted and sweaty, I keep thinking about Emma. How she looked the other night when I pulled back from kissing her, her hair a mess and her cheeks warm. She gripped my jacket and pulled me close, her big green eyes holding secrets that I can't even begin to guess at.

For a second, she was every man's fantasy. And for a second, I almost let her pull me back in.

But I didn't.

Now I'm stripping to shower, and standing under the water, and wondering why. I mean, I know why. Asher has put one restriction on our friendship, and that's Emma.

But a little voice in the back of my head says, so what?

So you owe Asher forever. So he put the only girl that you're interested in out of bounds. So doing anything with her will make you the worst, most ungrateful friend ever.

I stand under the steaming shower, and decide to let myself forget the rules for just a minute. Instead, I focus on what Emma tastes like, the soft little moans she makes, the way her curves feel under my hands. I'm hard in no time, my soapy hand running down to my cock. I give myself one solitary stroke, from root to tip, and groan aloud.

There is no doubt that I'm hard up for Emma. I have been for a few years, ever since I noticed her tits one night when we were all hanging out together. One minute I was drinking a beer, another minute I was fixating on her. Wondering what they looked like, how they would fit in the palms of my hands... wondering how they would taste.

I shiver, my body running hot and cold, just thinking about it. But I'm not allowed to touch, not allowed to find out just what the texture would be beneath my tongue. I'm frustrated, that much is obvious. But a solution to my problem is not forthcoming.

I run through the rest of my showering routine in a couple of minutes. Turning off the spigot and wrapping a towel around my waist, I open the door to the steam filled bathroom. I head down the hall to my bedroom, passing Asher's open door. He's not home, which is just as well.

What would I even say to him at this point?

When I get to my room, I notice the door is slightly ajar. That's a little weird, because I am always careful to close it all the way. Edging it open fully, I am greeted by the sight of Emma, stripped down to her matching red lace bra and panties... in my bed.

My eyebrows couldn't raise any higher. I clench the towel around my waist.

"Hi," she says shyly, even though she's fucking half naked in my bed. Her hair is pinned up, and she's just laying in my bed as though it's perfectly natural.

"What the hell are you doing here?" I grit out, glancing behind me.

Emma tilts her head. "Asher's gone. I thought... you and I could... um... *you* know..."

"You thought that since your brother is busy, you'd just come over here and I would fuck you?" I ask flatly.

She makes a face. "No, not exactly. But also... kind of."

I point to the door. "No way. Get out."

She looks timid for a moment, before she bites her lip and shakes her head.

"I don't think so. I don't think you really want me to go."

"Oh, so you're an expert now in what I want?" I cock my brow.

She flushes a deep dusty pink. "I want to be, if you'll let me."

"I think you should leave," I argue, hitching my towel up. "Seriously, Emma. You don't know what you're doing."

"I think... I think I do," she says.

Her green eyes glint a little in the low light of the bedside lamp. She slowly gets on her knees on the middle of my bed, starting to unhook her bra. I do a double take, glancing behind me at the open door. I close it, in case Ashter comes home.

"Emma, don't do—" I start. But then her bra is off, her fucking incredible breasts bare before me. As I stare, openmouthed, her perfect pink nipples pebble while I watch, tightening. I start to feel my cock harden underneath my towel.

I want to tell her to stop, to put her bra back on... but all I do is take a step toward her, staring in fascination. Her tits are just... amazing. She brings her hands up to her ribcage, teasing herself... and teasing me at the same time.

God *damn*. She is so fucking hot, I can't even stand it.

"Mmmm," she says, closing her eyes. "It feels so good."

She runs her hands up over both of her tits, her fingers squeezing her pouty pink nipples. I'm frozen in place, unable to make her leave or join her. She opens her eyes a little.

"If you come closer, I promise to keep my hands to myself..." She bites her lip. "Really."

She moves over a little, making room on my bed.

"I... I can't. I don't trust myself," I admit, my voice gone to gravel.

Emma looks at me for a second. "Can I tell you something private?"

My brows lower. "We're mostly naked, alone in my bedroom. I would hope that whatever you have to say, you could say it to me."

She blushes again, lowering her voice. "I... I've never... orgasmed before, at least not with anyone else. I want— I want to know what it's like. I want... I want..."

She's so raw, so vulnerable in that moment. How can I resist her, of all people, asking me this, of all things?

I don't speak, but I come around the side of the bed. She's like a moth to a flame, fluttering where I go. She comes to the side of the bed. Even kneeling, she still so fucking tiny compared to me.

Our eyes meet, both of us staring intensely, trying to take the other's measure.

Her lips part. "Please, Jameson..."

I reach out, my hand shaking a little with the intensity of the moment. I run my fingertips over her delicate collarbone, her gently sloping shoulder. My hand dwarfs her body with ease. She's so breakable, so easily damaged. It has never been so apparent as it is now, when she's on her knees before me, her green eyes searching my face.

I lean down, brushing my lips ever so gently at the corner of her mouth.

"I can't promise to be nice," I whisper. "I can't say that I will take it easy on you."

The excitement that darkens her eyes as I say it... that doesn't bode well for me. Emma is too easily damaged for me to do all the things I really want to do. I have to remember that.

"Do it," she whispers, taking my hand and drawing it upward until it rests around the slim column of her throat. "Please. I'm begging you."

Fuck. Is there anything I've wanted more than to see a naked Emma on her knees, begging for me to fuck her?

I tighten my hand for just a second, feeling her breath quicken. Then I turn my head, nipping at her lower lip. Her breath leaves her in a *whoosh*. I descend on her mouth, moving to kneel on the bed. I kiss her hard, snaking my tongue out to meet hers. Her hands land on my hips, her touch tentative.

I stop, pull back. "Don't touch me," I order. "I'll do all the touching."

She bites her lip, her hands leaving my hips. I bend to kiss her again, my hands coming up to trace the lines of her face, her neck. I shape her tits with my hands, stifling a groan. They are the perfect handfuls, a little small but so fucking perky, the nipples standing out. My mouth waters, I want to taste them so badly.

I push her backward until she collapses onto the bed, falling onto a huge pile of pillows. She struggles to sit up, but I lean into her a little, holding her down. I feel my towel give way, and I let it come loose. My cock juts out, so fucking hard, but I do my best to ignore it.

I dip my head lower, pushing one nipple up with a hand, taking the most delicate taste. My lips find her nipple, and the contact makes her groan aloud.

God, she fucking tastes like honey. I make a noise deep in my throat, sucking in more of her flesh. Both of her hands hit the bed, digging into the comforter as she makes these tiny, breathy sounds.

"Oh, oh, oh, *oh*," she says. It's music to my fucking ears.

I release her breast from my mouth with a pop. I know where else I have to taste. I've been dreaming of the taste of her pussy for three years. Now's my fucking chance, and I don't want to wait any more. I want my tongue to explore her every crevice, to make her squirm, to make her *scream*...

"Panties off," I command. I am done with waiting. "Quick."

Emma hurries to hook two fingers in the waistband of her panties. She only now seems to realize that my cock has been freed from my towel, and she looks at me with her eyes gone wide. Maybe she she's never seen such a big cock before. Regardless, I don't have time for her to gawk.

Impatient, I lean over and grab her panties, yanking them down her legs. I toss them aside, my gaze riveted on the thin strip of hair that leads down to her pussy. My cock stands at attention as I reach out to smooth my touch across her stomach and her hipbones.

I stand up, stroking my cock for a second. I enjoy looking down at her, seeing her blush, seeing her attempts to cover herself with her hands. I want her wild and wanton, her head thrown back as she enjoys herself a little. I want to see her toes curl, I want to be the name that she calls out when she's about to cum.

I want it all, and I want to remember it forever.

So I stifle my impatience and pull her knees to the edge of the bed. "Have you fantasized about this? About me, fucking you until you scream?"

Emma's eyes go wide. She looks up at me, her eyes alight with anticipation. "Y-yes.."

I squeeze her knee. "Dirty girl. I want you to show me exactly what you do when you think of me. Touch your tits, spread those legs. I want to see you play with your clit."

She flushes bright red, which I love. "Jameson…"

"Do what I ask, and I will finish you off with my mouth. I am desperate for a taste of that pussy." I issue it as a challenge and offer it like a reward, but I know that it's really me that will be enjoying her reward. I wait with bated breath for her to decide.

She takes the bait. Closing her eyes, she bites her lower lip and caresses both of her tits, pulling them each to a fine point.

"Fuck," I utter. "You're so fucking hot, Emma. I like the way you play with your tits."

My cock demands attention, so I give my cock a gentle stroke, tip to root. I'm so sensitive right now, watching Emma as she tentatively spreads her thighs. When she reveals her perfectly pink pussy, already glistening with her juices, I slow my touch even more.

Normally I would just go as hard as possible, balls to the wall, but I'm almost sure that I'll spill before she does. I don't want that.

As I watch, she spreads her pussy wide with two fingers, exposing her clit to me. I bite my lower lip. She uses her other hand to gently brush the pad of a finger over her clit. Her brow puckers, her eyes closed hard.

I can't decide where I should be looking, and my eyes keep bouncing around from her tits back to her pussy.

"Mmm, it feels good," she murmurs. "I won't last very long."

That, I think, is my cue. I kneel at the edge of the bed, resting my hands on the insides of her thighs. Her eyes open like a lazy cat's, so green that they pin me in place for a second. I bend down and brush a kiss on the inside of her knee.

Her fingers keep working, slowly caressing her clit. I trail my lips up toward her pussy, listening to her soft sighs, pushing her thighs open more and more. Finally I close my lips over her clit, pushing away her hands. She tastes fucking incredible. Just like honey, with a deeper undertone of musk and excitement.

"Ohhhh *god*," she says. "That feels so damn good."

I alternate between sucking rhythmically and swirling my tongue around her clit. I draw her legs over my shoulders, and she starts moving against my mouth, hungry for more. She grows vocal all of the sudden, little *oh*s and *mmm*s pouring out of her mouth, her head thrown back into the pillows.

This, this moment is exactly what I wanted. My cock aches, more than ready to be inside her. But I ignore it, focusing on Emma, on what she so clearly wants and needs right now. I swirl my tongue, thinking about whether or not to introduce my fingers to the mix.

It's too late for that, though. She stiffens, bearing down, and I know she's going to come even before she says it.

"Oh god… oh god, I'm going to… FUCK! Jameson!!"

She comes in pulses, writhing against my tongue. Hearing my name on her lips when she's at the brink feels good, though of course I am right here… I'm face level with her clenching, needy pussy. I know that I could stand up and plunge inside her, that thrusting all the way in would satisfy the soul-deep ache that Emma causes.

It would wreck me, probably. Wreck us both, maybe forever.

I'm very, very tempted. God knows, we both want it enough.

I continue swirling my tongue gently until she pulls away,

too sensitive for any more contact. Then I carefully disentangle myself from her. She reaches for me, and I give her a long, deep kiss.

One of her hands brushes my cock, hesitant. I close my eyes, picturing what would happen if I allowed her to pull me down, if I let her touch my aching cock. I imagine my release, our shared release, would be so amazing...

My phone starts to ring though, and I yank myself back. What the hell am I doing?

"Wait—" she begins to say.

"I think it would be better if you left," I say in a strangled voice. "I should... I should go shower."

I look around for my towel, growing frantic. What have I done? There's no way to undo this, not now. I find my towel, and use it to cover my cock.

"But you just came from the shower!" she says, confused. "Why are you being weird all the sudden?"

I take several steps back towards the door. I look at Emma, her cheeks dark pink and her hair wild.

"This was... we can't do this," I manage. "We just can't."

That's all I can say. I rip open my door and throw myself down the hall, until I'm safely behind the bathroom door again.

Stupid, stupid, *stupid*! I think. This is really fucked, now. Asher officially has the grounds to never speak to me again.

I sink onto the bathroom floor, hoping like hell that Emma will just go. I just can't explain my chaotic thinking to her when I leave this room.

I lick my lips, the taste of her still on my lips, like a burning brand.

What have I done?

16

EMMA

"Remember, the very foundation of due process is truth..." the professor says. He's sitting in front of my law school class, talking animatedly about constitutional law. He's a white guy, probably about sixty five years old, with wild white hair and a rumpled suit. "Anyway, back to your final exam..."

I sit at my desk, tapping my pen on my open notebook, and suppress a sigh. This is my very last class before my finals, which will take place over the next two days. I should definitely be paying attention to what Dr. Smith is saying...

Instead, I'm focused on Jameson. This is nothing new, really. I've probably never sat through an entire high school, college, or law school class period without at least thinking of him.

But now there's new fuel for the bonfire that is my imagination. Memories, fresh from two days ago... and they're hot, too. Images of us kissing, of the naughty things he made me do, of him feasting on my pussy like it was his only job...

I'm getting a little wet, sitting here thinking about it.

Of course, as amazing as it all was, things could've ended on a better note. Jameson ended up... what should I say? Not freaking out, exactly. He wasn't panicking, but he told me very clearly that what we were doing was wrong.

I know his reasons. He's too much older than me, my brother

will kill him, he's from the wrong side of the tracks... blah blah blah. I know them, and I still don't care.

He's too late, anyway. Because now I know without a doubt that Jameson wants me almost as bad as I want him...

And I do want him. I want him in my bed, dominating me. I want him on my tiny kitchen table, halfway standing up, real quick. I want him to take me in the ocean, as slow and steady as the waves.

I've always wanted Jameson. I've only wanted *him*.

The thing is, now that we both know that there are sparks flying between us, I need a little more from him. I have tried turning up in his bed, half dressed. Now it's his turn to show me that he wants me...

And I haven't the slightest idea how that is going to happen. I think about this weekend with a sigh. They're hosting a French DJ this weekend at Cure, having him spin all weekend, so I guess I know exactly where Jameson will be.

Behind the bar of Cure, trying not to look at Asher directly, probably. I sigh aloud, drawing the gaze of a couple other students.

I realize that the students around me are standing up and gathering their things. Getting up and shoving my textbooks into my satchel, I start to leave the classroom. I'm one of the last people to go, but I stop abruptly near the doorway.

I blink owlishly at Brad, a well groomed blond guy who's been in my study group for the whole semester. Brad smiles nervously at me, blocking the door.

"Hey, Emma," he says.

Even though he says my name, I look to my left, wondering for a second if he means to talk to me. Maybe he wants to study or something, but usually those conversations only happen via the class-wide message board. I don't think we've actually ever spoken.

"Uhhh... yeah?" I say, hugging my satchel closer.

"I was thinking... I mean, I was wondering if you wanted to celebrate tonight? It being the last day of classes and all."

My eyebrows rise. "Err... what?"

He flushes bright red. "The whole study group was talking before class about going out tonight. You know, to party before we get serious about hitting the books. I wanted to know if you wanted to come with us."

I pause, my mouth ajar. I know what he's asking. Brad is asking me out, but he's too shy to just come out with it. The devil on my shoulder rubs her hands and cackles with glee, because Brad is so... *normal*.

From his Dockers to his perfectly bland beige button up, Jameson would loathe everything about this guy on principal.

I shouldn't do it, but I ask: "Where were you thinking? Because I know a place that's having this French DJ tonight..."

And Brad, poor innocent Brad, just grins. "That sounds great! I mean, you know, I will have to run it by the others..."

"Uh huh," I say, digging for a pen and a notebook in my satchel. "Here, this is the name of the bar... shall we say around nine?"

"Yeah, totally. That sounds really amazing." Brad is still blushing.

I narrow my eyes. "You know, my roommate Evie would like you. She's a total knockout, and she likes guys who are kinda shy. I'll have to bring her tonight."

Brad's eyes widen. "Umm... okay?"

"Great. I'll see you then," I say with a smile. "That is, if you let me get out."

"What? Oh! Yeah, haha." He steps aside, and I head out the door. "See you tonight!"

I wave half-heartedly over my shoulder. I know that it's probably wrong to use Brad like this, knowing that I don't intend to go home with him... but I still shiver as I think of how Jameson will react, seeing me flaunting myself with another guy.

My bet is it will drive him insane, seeing what *should* be his in Brad's hands.

There's only one way to find out, though. I head home, my mind full of plans.

17

EMMA

I glance at Evie, who's completely outdone herself, wearing a dark lace two piece. Her hair is pinned up in an elegant updo, on the miles of coffee-and-cream bare skin that she shows off... she's nothing short of stunning.

"Do I look okay?" she asks, checking her dark red lipstick out in a compact she pulls from her purse.

I grin as we cross the boardwalk by Cure. "You look like a model, bitch. Everyone is going to be staring at you all night."

"Speak for yourself, Miss *I'm Wearing Half A Minidress*. That guy is going to have a freaking stroke when he sees you," she says.

"What guy?"

"The one who asked you to this thing. I don't think he was ready for you to show up in a black Versace dress that is so tiny, if you even lean over, we're all gonna know what kind of underpants you prefer."

I grin. "You know that I'm not dressed up for Brad."

Evie rolls her pretty chocolate-colored eyes. "I know. I'm just saying..."

We get to the smooth dark glass windows of Cure, and I can already feel the vibrations from the music leaking out the windows. "Come on, I want to see what they've done with the place. Asher said that he was going to decorate the bar tonight."

I tow Evie by the wrist, opening the door. Immediately, the music overwhelms me like a flood. It's high energy club music, a persistent whub dub dub underlying various vocals. As I step into the darkened bar, I see that it's already packed with people.

"Oooh, look!" Evie says, pointing to the decor. Asher has put up mirrors on nearly every conceivable surface, and between that and the lights, everything is flashing and reflective. There is even a multicolored and reflective DJ booth set up at the far end, by the bathrooms and the door to the patio.

"Let's get a drink," I say, pulling Evie toward the end of the bar.

We skirt several large groups of people who are laughing and trying to talk over the music, scooting in at the empty space at the very end of the bar. It looks like Gunnar, Asher, and Jameson are all working behind the bar.

I stand on my tiptoes to see Jameson a little better, but my line of sight is soon blocked by Gunnar.

"Holy shit," he says, looking at me and Evie with wide eyes. "You guys both look..."

He whistles, or I think he does. It's hard to hear anything above the music. I lean in close to make myself heard.

"Thanks!" I say, wiggling my eyebrows. "Can we get a drink?"

"Yeah. Anything in particular?"

I shake my head. "You know what I like. And make four drinks, because I need a little alcohol in my body, stat."

Gunnar grins. "Gotcha, Emma."

He turns to make our drinks. I see Jameson, looking tall and handsome and definitely surly as he makes drinks. He looks up and sees me, and then scowls. I roll my eyes, spinning to look around the bar. Let him see me, not caring what he thinks.

I spot Brad and a few people from my study group, standing awkwardly in the corner. It's pretty much what I expected of the group, honestly. When Gunnar brings the drinks, I toast him.

I hand the other drink to Evie, who takes the tiniest sip. "Ugh, this is horrible. Maybe I just need a water"

"Seriously? Bitch, I got you two drinks," I say. Tipping my head back, I drink the first drink in a few gulps. I make a face at the overpowering taste of fruit punch. It's followed by something darker, probably whatever kind of liquor is in there. "Yuck."

"Don't be a baby, I'm just not entirely over this stomach bug," Evie says. She puts her her glass down on the bar. "It just means more drinks for you. Now, where are your friends?"

I nod in the direction of the group. "Over there."

Evie doesn't even pause. She just strides over to them, leaving me to follow after her. She singles Brad and another guy out, introducing herself.

"Hey!" she shouts, leaning in. "I'm Evie, Emma's roommate!"

Brad looks to me, and I swear to god he swallows his own tongue. He sputters, unable to form a coherent thought. I smirk. I must look good, then.

Smiling, I walk up to him. "You made it!"

Brad is blushing furiously. He steps a little closer to me, leaning in to be heard. "Yeah, I did for sure. This place is really hip. How'd you find it?"

"I wish I could claim the credit, but it's actually my brother's place. He owns it." I think of Jameson, brooding behind the bar. "Well, my brother and his best friend."

That makes Brad nervous. He looks behind me. "Err... does that mean your brother is here?"

"Yeah. Let's see..." I turn around, looking for Asher. I accidentally make eye contact with Jameson, and wince a little. J's expression is dark as a thundercloud before a storm... and he's looking right at me, too.

"That's your brother?" Brad says, nodding in Jameson's direction. Jameson turns away, focusing on making drinks.

"Uhhh... no," I say, shaking my head. "There, behind the bar, in the middle? That's my brother."

Asher is arguing with Gunnar over something, not even aware that I'm here.

"Huh." Brad looks relieved. "I thought that maybe your brother was one of those guys who thinks that his little sister needs protection or something."

I glance at Jameson again, who is furiously pouring whiskey

into a cocktail shaker. He's trying so hard not to look at me that it seems more obvious than when he was staring right at me.

I smother a triumphant expression. He does care, a heck of a lot more than he lets on. Well, let him glare all he wants. He can stop my flirting with Brad anytime he wants with just a few words.

I turn back to Brad. "Do you want to dance?"

Brad's eyebrows fly up, and he clears his throat. "With you?"

I roll my eyes, taking a gulp of my drink. I shudder at the taste, but I know it will help loosen me up.

"Come on!" I shout. "Pretend you're having fun, okay?"

I grab him by the arm, pulling him out into the middle of the room. I'm not the first one to have the idea to dance. There are a few couples dancing already. I throw myself into Brad's arms, dancing wildly at first. Poor Brad tries to awkwardly dance along, but he mostly throws off my rhythm.

We dance through five songs, and we're both sweaty by the second one. I make sure to turn toward the bar every now and then, just to make sure that Jameson is still directing his glare my way.

I pretend not to notice him, shimmying and getting cozy in Brad's arms.

"Wow, you are a really good dancer!" Brad says in my ear. "I feel lucky that you picked me to dance with."

"Oh... thanks," I say, cringing inside.

I feel a pang of guilt for essentially using Brad to make Jameson jealous. I bite my lip, slowing down. I did tell him earlier that I would introduce him to Evie, but looking around I have no idea where she has gone.

I decide that being direct is probably the best approach.

"Hey," I say, leaning close. "I'm um... I have a crush on someone else. I'm sorry, it's probably crappy of me not to have come right out and said anything."

Brad's expression is mortified, mixed with a look like I just kicked his favorite puppy right in the face. "You... what? Really?"

Chewing on my lower lip, I nod. "Yeah."

"Wait, why come at all if you weren't interested?" he says, confused.

"To make someone jealous," I admit. "I know, I'm terrible. But I can make it up to you! Pick any other girl here, and I'll be your wingman."

Several emotions play across Brad's face, but he seems resigned to his fate. "Yeah, alright. You should have told me, though. I could've pulled off some more dramatic moves."

I frown. "Like what?"

"Like…" He grabs me by the waist without notice, dips me so I fall backward, and plants the biggest kiss right on my lips. When he lets me up, he grins. "There's more where that came from. Not too late to change your mind, you know."

I laugh. "Good to know…"

Out of the corner of my eye, I see Jameson ripping his apron off over his head and throwing it down on the counter. We make eye contact for a second, and he glares at me furiously, muttering to himself.

He comes out from behind the bar and storms toward the patio. I look at Brad, who still looks at me vaguely hopefully. I can't just leave him hanging.

I look around, and spot a pretty blonde about our age who is standing alone and texting. I leave Brad and go up to her.

"Hey!" I shout.

She looks up at me, startled. "Yes?"

"My friend over there?" I say, pointing to Brad. "He thinks you're mega cute, but he's too shy to say hello. Will you come talk to him?"

She blushes and looks at Brad, taking a second to think it over. "Yeah, alright…"

"Great! You won't be sorry." I grin at her, motioning her to follow me. I get back to Brad, who has been watching the whole exchange with a distrustful expression.

"Brad, this is…" I stop, realizing I don't know her name.

"Gisella," she supplies helpfully.

"Cool name! Gisella, this is Brad. You two should talk!" I put a hand on both of their backs, urging them to move closer together. "I'll be right back!"

While they're starting to shake hands and introduce themselves, I make my dash for the patio. I bob and weave to avoid people on the dance floor, pushing open the door. As the door closes behind me, the music fades to a faint whub whub sound.

I look around at the tables on the patio, most of which are empty. No Jameson in sight, so I head to the very back of the patio. There's a little rickety gate that lets me out into the back of the building, where there is a little alley between Cure and the employee parking lot.

I find Jameson there, leaning against the wall and staring at a cigarette longingly. He's so tall and big that he sort of dwarfs everything that happens to be behind him, a dumpster included. When he looks over and sees me coming, he pushes off the wall. He throws the cigarette away in the dumpster, scowling.

"I didn't know you smoked," I say, stopping a few feet from him. I run a hand over my minidress, as if it needs me to draw attention it it. Jameson looks at me for a second, seeming tormented.

Just how I want him.

"Yeah, well. There's a whole lot you don't know about me," he growls, looking away. "Now piss off. I'm on my break."

I cock my hip. "You want to send me back to dance with Brad?"

If I thought I'd seen him glower at me before, I was clearly wrong. The way he looks at me right now, all seething and dark… that is exactly how I hoped he would stare at me. He's looking at me with those dark, sexy eyes of his…

It's all I can do not to melt right here, right now.

"What do you want from me?" he asks. The way he says it is aggressive, which is odd given his choice of words. He moves closer, and goosebumps break out over my arms. "What would you have me do, Emma?"

I move a step closer, bringing us nearly face to face. He's so much taller than me, I have to crane my head to look up at him. I bite my lip, reaching out and running a fingertip up his arm.

"You know what I want," I say, looking into his eyes. He looks at me with such torment, so much fiery hunger, that I think I'm going to combust. "I want *you*."

Apparently those were the magic words, because Jameson breaks, his arms pulling me close, his mouth descending onto mine. He whirls and pins me up against the stucco wall, putting his knee between my legs and lifting me a little. I open my mouth to him, and he completely takes control of the kiss, rough and dominant in the way that I crave.

The wall is rough against my back, but I barely even notice. I'm so caught up in the feeling of Jameson pressed against me, the sensation of his tongue toying with mine, his big hand climbing my thigh.

He releases my mouth, only to bite my neck, and I groan loudly. When he discovers that I'm not wearing any panties, he moans softly.

"Fuck, Emma," he whispers. His fingers trace their way inward from my hip to find my pussy already soaking wet for him. He searches for my clit for a second, sucking on my neck in a sweet spot.

Then he finds my clit, and I actually see stars for a second. Then he slides one thick finger inside me, and I make a strangled sound. He groans a little.

"God *damn*, you're tight," he murmurs into my ear.

I want to say, that's because I'm still a virgin. But I don't. Either he knows that or he doesn't, but either way it's not really the time to discuss that. It does make me realize that unless I want my first time to be right here, with my back against the rough stucco wall, I'd better say something.

Do I want to say something?

He moves his finger inside me, working my clit at the same time, and I have to gasp for breath. If I'm going to say something, now is the time.

I kiss him, slowly pushing him away at the same time. He

growls and presses me back against the wall, and I have to actually speak up.

"Stop," I plead quietly.

Instantly he stills, then backs up, looking betrayed. "I thought—"

"Shh, no. I know. I just... I want it in a bed," I say, turning red. "If there were no one else around, maybe here would be fine..."

Understanding dawns on his face, and he looks a little ashamed of himself.

"Oh. I mean, of course."

I reach out and grab him by the back of his neck, kissing him long and slow, until we're both out of breath. "I do want you. I do."

Jameson kisses me again, then backs away. "I have to work the rest of my shift. I can't just leave."

I look at him, willing myself to have the nerve to ask him to my place. "Come to my house tonight, after you're done here. I promise, you won't be disappointed."

He is so hesitant, it's almost heartbreaking. "All right."

"You'll really come over?"

He pauses for the longest moment, then nods. "Yeah."

I smile at him, feeling my face burn. "Okay. I'll be ready for you."

He glances over his shoulder, back towards the bar. "All right. Go, before I change my mind."

I honestly don't know if he means that he would change his mind about coming over or if he means he would insist on having sex in this alley. He turns and heads back to the bar, and I am left to walk down the alley.

18

EMMA

I glance at the clock on my bedside table for maybe the thousandth time. It's 12:31 am, and I am sprawled on my bed, still waiting for Jameson. I've done everything I can to make the bedroom sexier... I've lit candles, shaved my legs again, and I even have a sexy playlist on repeat. All that's missing is Jameson.

Tugging down the bottom of my black silk slip, I wonder when I should start thinking that he isn't coming. I mean, he said he was going to come, but what if something happened? What if he had to deal with something at the bar that will keep him all night?

Or even worse, what if he changes his mind about wanting me? What if he did the math, and my brother's stupid rule suddenly outweighs the desire Jameson feels for me?

Maybe I was stupid to stop him back there in the alley. It felt important then, but maybe it really was—

Thunk. The sound of the front door closing makes me jump. I sit up on my bed. Is it Jameson after all?

When I hear his heavy footsteps in the hall, slow and deliberate, goosebumps break out across my flesh. It's him. He's really here... and he's coming for me.

I try to still my racing heartbeat, taking slow sips of air. The bedroom door slowly opens to reveal Jameson. He fills up the doorframe, in his leather jacket and dark jeans. His energy is brooding, almost angry… and it turns me on as much as it makes me nervous.

I feel his brown-black eyes staring me down, raking over every inch of me almost like a physical touch. He doesn't say anything for a minute, he just stands there, looking at me. I want to cover myself, to hide from his gaze, but I don't.

"You came," I say, coming up on my knees.

"I shouldn't have." He grips the door frame while he just looks at me. His expression is that of a man who's starving, who is desperate for something… and I'm chilled to think that what he's desperate for is *me*.

"But you did." He's going to need some more convincing, it seems. I bite my lower lip and use two fingers to tug one of my slip's straps over my shoulder, making eye contact with him the whole time. "Come here, Jameson. Touch me. *Please.*"

My heart is about to beat right out of my chest. He steps forward, closing the door with his foot.

Yes. I'm about to get what I want, finally.

Jameson takes off his leather jacket, slinging it aside. I move to the edge of my bed, more eager for him than I want to admit. He moves closer until we're just a hair's breadth apart, looking down at me, his dark eyes searching my face. He brings his face close to mine, avoiding my mouth, and whispers in my ear.

"You really want this?" he asks softly. My breath leaves me in a *whoosh*. His **scruff** touches my cheek.

I nod, swallowing. "I want *you*."

He brushes my hair back with two fingers. Then he slides his big hand around my neck ever so slowly, and gives my neck a light squeeze.

"You know I won't be gentle with you, right? I've thought about this too much, fantasized about you too often to go easy on you." He turns his head ever so slightly, and places a single kiss on my neck.

I shiver convulsively, only able to nod. I have waited for him for years, There's nothing that he could say that will make me change my mind.

He moves back to look at me, and I see the fire raging in his eyes. A fire that I feel too, a fire that could consume us both for all I care. His gaze drops to my lips, and I lean forward, lips parting. He moves to kiss me, his lips firm and demanding.

This is no peck on the lips. His tongue invades my mouth, sweeping and exploring. My tongue dances with his as I sigh and sink into it.

Curling my hand around the back of his neck, I reach out boldly with my free hand and grasp his hip. He allows it for a second, then breaks off the kiss and pushes me back onto the bed.

"Stay there," he orders me.

He begins to undress, taking off his shoes, pulling his tee shirt off over his head. His torso ripples as he does, and I admire his light dusting of dark chest hair. He's also got a trail of hair that leads down from his belly button and disappears into his waistband. His arms flex as he unzips his jeans, but he stops there.

I get a tantalizing peek into his unbuttoned pants as he comes closer, just for a second.

He moves onto the bed, kneeling at the end. He considers me for a moment, like he's trying to decide what to do with me. "Come here."

I shiver as I move closer, feeling like I'm under a microscope. He narrows his eyes and runs a single fingertip across my collarbone, down under the remaining strap of my slip. He draws the strap off of my shoulder, and then rolls the top of the slip down until my pink nipples are exposed to the air.

"I've imagined this a hundred times," he says absently, his eyes fixed on my nipples. "But there is no comparison to the way you actually taste."

He leans down, cupping one breast and pulling the nipple to his mouth. I immediately groan at the sensation of his hot, wet mouth on my flesh. He rolls it around with his tongue, then bites it very carefully, almost like he's testing me.

"Ahh!" I gasp. "You can do it harder."

He smirks, looking up at me. "Permission noted."

Then he elbows me aside, lying down. I look at him a little quizzically, but in the next second he lifts me onto his body, so that I'm straddling him. He angles me so that he's planted face first between my breasts, and my bare ass is in the air. I'm a little shocked at how easily he picked me up, but he clearly has other things on his mind.

He licks the skin between my breasts with his tongue, then pulls one nipple into his mouth. I moan as he bites it and sucks it, alternating pain and pleasure for me. His hands wander down to my hips, bunching up my slip. He runs his hands over my ass, groaning when he finds that I am bare underneath the slip.

He releases my breast with a wet pop, looking up at me. "*Fuck*. You're not wearing any panties. Do you know how much that turns me on?"

I blush, slowly shaking my head. "Uh uh."

He pushes my hips down until my pussy is pressed directly against his cock through his unbuttoned jeans. We both groan as he bucks up against me. He runs his hand through my hair, fisting it, and uses his hand on my hip to guide me just where he wants me.

I gasp silently as he lifts his hips and bears down on me, his denim-clad cock almost touching my clit. He starts kissing and licking my neck, using my hair as a tool to move my head to his liking. He sucks the spot where my neck meets my shoulder, bucking his hips up, and my eyes roll back into my head.

"Fuck!" I cry. "Jameson—"

He's not satisfied with that, though. He releases me, pushing me off of his lap. I'm left breathing hard. He gets up and starts to peel his jeans off.

"Clothes *off*," he commands. I instantly obey, starving for more of what I know he's going to give me. Lifting my arms over my head, I raise the slip up and over my head.

When I get the slip off, I'm taken aback for a moment by the image of Jameson, completely naked. He's all muscle, his cock juts proud out… and right now, he's looking at me like he's going to consume me.

He cocks his head for a second, holding something up. A

condom. He crinkles the wrapper, tearing it, and rolls it on like a pro. I'm on an IUD, so I don't really need the condom, but it's very much appreciated.

He climbs onto the bed, dragging me down to lie beneath him, and he starts kissing my neck again. I wrap my arms and legs around him, pulling him closer. I can feel his hardness against my thigh, long and hot and throbbing. He sucks at my neck, my breasts, and then he moves lower.

I don't know if I can even handle his mouth on my clit, but he passionately kisses my thighs and my knees. His scruff tickles in the best way. I open my legs wide for him, spreading my thighs. He makes a growling sound as he kisses my clit, and my whole body is suddenly alive with electric sensation.

"Oh my god!" I cry out, my hands burying in his hair.

Already, I'm bucking my hips against his mouth, desperate for more. He closed his mouth around my clit and sucks on it in long pulls, each one sending ripples of sensation up my spine. My toes curl as he brings his hand up to my pussy and introduces one thick finger. He ever so slowly pushes his finger inside as he circles my clit with his tongue.

I come suddenly, clenching and crying out. His tongue slows, helping me ride out my orgasm. Soon though, he climbs up my body, kissing me hard. I taste the faint flavor of my own juices on his tongue and shudder.

He pulls back a little bit, grasping his cock and positioning himself just so. The blunt tip of his cock presses against my pussy, and I still for just a second. I'm busy looking at his cock, trying to understand how the hell it's going to fit inside me. He pushes inside the barest inch. I cry out from pleasure and pain all at once.

Jameson glances down at me, biting his lip. "You're so tight, Em."

I'm honestly not sure if that's a good thing or not, judging by his face alone. He looks like he's trying to defuse a bomb or something. I wrap my legs around his hips, pulling at him a little, urging him onward.

He closes his eyes and pushes himself inside, inch by slow

inch. I feel like he's stretching me out, little by little, filling me up and touching every single part of me. It's uncomfortable, even though I'm wet. Maybe due to his size, or maybe due to the fact that I've never been penetrated before.

When he is finally inside me to the hilt, he opens his eyes, staring down at me with the most intense black-brown gaze I've ever experienced.

I look him right in the eye, realizing in that moment that I'm in love with him. I don't care that his dick is so big that it hurts a little; I'm too busy being stupidly, dumbly in love with Jameson.

I reach up to pull his mouth down to mine, tenderly kissing him. He kisses me back, starting to move his body, withdrawing his cock and then thrusting back in.

"Ahhh, that's so good," he mutters, raising himself up so that he can see our bodies joined together. "Fuck, Emma. God, you're so damned beautiful."

He grabs my wrists and pulls them up above my head, working his thick cock in and out. I dig my heels into his upper back as he starts kissing and biting my neck again. I start to forget the discomfort, focusing instead on the pleasure of his lips on my skin, the wonderful weight of his body against mine.

I moan as he releases my hands in order to palm my breasts. It feels natural to wrap my arms around him, to lightly rake my fingernails down his back.

Jameson suddenly withdraws from me, flipping me over. He guides me to my hands and knees, positioning his cock at my entrance before he plunges back inside.

"Ohhh!" I cry out, feeling my innermost muscles clench.

"Your pussy feels so good," he grits out. He takes my hand and guides it down to my clit, rubbing it in gentle circles. "I want you to come again. Show me what a good girl you are. Make yourself come for me."

His words send a shudder of pleasure down my spine. He lets go of my hand and grabs my hips, thrusting his cock into me again and again, as hard as he can. I call out, an insensible sound, as I start to touch myself.

The way he is fucking me now is rougher, coarser than

before... but for some reason I like it more. A lot more. I close my eyes, rubbing my clit, and feeling the brutal way he handles me, ramming into me over and over again.

An invisible spring tightens deep inside me with every thrust, feeding my craving. My fingers help me along, but it's really J's cock that makes little ripples of pleasure swell and burst across my body.

He's touching some spot deep inside me, a spot that I seem to be able to angle my body just so to encourage him to hit over and over again.

"Yes," I groan desperately. "Yes, right there... I..."

And then I'm calling out his name, screaming it, as I go over the edge, falling into a deep ocean of pleasure. He stiffens and growls, filling me with three single, brutal thrusts. I can feel him pulsing inside my pussy.

He slows at last, half-collapsing on the bed with me. He turns me over, kissing me tenderly. I cling to him, feeling...

Loved? Freshly fucked? Overwhelmed?

Whatever else, I feel thoroughly deflowered. I lay on his chest, listening to his rapid heartbeat as it begins to slow. I'm trying to figure out how to ask him to stay, but he just lies there, stroking my arm, not seeming to be in any rush to leave.

My eyelids begin to droop, and my breathing evens out. I'm not asleep per se, but I'm not far from it. When he speaks, it startles me.

"Ready to go again?" he asks, his voice barely more than a rumble in his chest.

I open my eyes and squint at him. "Again?"

He chuckles, brushing my hair back from my neck. He places a long, lazy kiss on my bare skin. "I said I wasn't going to go easy on you, didn't I?"

I bite my lip, but we both already know my answer.

It's yes. It will always be yes, for him.

19

JAMESON

I fuck Emma three more times in the early hours of the morning, before I finally sleep a little. I didn't intend to fall asleep in her bed, but I'll admit to drowsing for a good couple of hours. After we fucked like a couple of horny teenagers, it was sort of inevitable.

When I wake up, I open my eyes to find Emma cuddled up against me. I look down at her sleeping face, and I have to take a breath. Emma is fucking gorgeous, not that I didn't already know that.

Her dark hair is fanned out away from her face, her nose just a little upturned, with a spray of delicate freckles. Her eyes are closed, long lashes resting lightly on her cheeks. Even asleep, her pouty lips are seductive, pulling me toward her face. Her brow is furrowed, like she's worried about something.

Looking down at her naked body, I can't help my response. The gentle slope of her ribs, the rise of her hips. Her beautiful fucking tits. And christ, those legs... just looking at them makes me remember them wrapped around my body while I thrust my cock into that amazing pussy of hers over and over again. I get a hard-on, a full blown one.

I try my best not to wake her as I slip my arm out from where it supports her head, but she stirs. Opening her eyes a little, she fuzzily focuses on me as I get dressed.

"You're going?" she asks softly, still mostly asleep.

Yeah, this is usually why I avoid sleeping over at a girl's place. I don't like answering all the questions that come after sex. In my experience, this is only the first of many questions to come. I sigh.

"Yeah," I say, pulling my pants on. "I should get back to my place."

"Mmm," she says, yawning. "It *is* almost dawn."

I give a look. "Yeah. I guess so."

Emma sits up a little more, pulling a blanket over herself. "Well... um... thanks, I guess. I doubt that anyone has ever lost their virginity so... *passionately*."

I freeze with my t-shirt halfway over my head. I definitely thought I heard her say virginity, but clearly I must be hearing things. I pull the shirt down over my head, frowning intensely at her.

"I'm sorry?"

She blushes. "I just mean... thanks for making my first time... special. You know, not in an alley, or whatever."

I don't surprise easily, but my mouth kind of hangs open for a second. I find it hard to speak. "I... I don't..."

Her brows rise. "You didn't... you're saying you didn't know?"

Jesus christ. Now the fact that I tried to have her in the alley behind Cure seems double extra trashy. I cringe as I think of how rough I was with her, every single time.

Fuck, is she thanking me as some sort of joke at my expense? I honestly don't even know.

"You could have told me," I grit out, grabbing my leather jacket off the floor. "Warned me, or whatever."

"I didn't think... I mean, I thought—" she stammers.

Fuck, Asher's going to kill me. If he wasn't going to before, he's definitely going to now. And what am I supposed to do with Emma now that I've taken her v card?

I know that I'm expected to do more than just leave her here, but it's too much pressure. I can't think like this. I have to get the fuck out of here, now.

"Whatever." I open her door, rushing out. Yeah, I'm that much of a coward. I leave without another word.

"Wait, Jameson…" she calls after me.

But I'm gone. I turn the corner, open her front door, and slam it behind me. I'm pissed, but not at Emma. I'm furious with myself, mostly. And a little with Asher, for good measure.

In the early light of dawn, I get outside of Emma's house and stomp over to my Jeep. I get in, but I don't start the car. I just sit for a minute, staring at the little bungalow. The sun is creeping up to the treetops, warming up the ancient blue paint on the eaves and casting long shadows across the sandy lawn.

For the life of me, I can't forget the look on her face when she told me I was her *first*. What the hell was I supposed to say to that?

Is it really possible to believe that I took Emma's virginity? I try to think back, to remember any serious boyfriends she's had… but I come up with nothing. As far as I can remember, she hasn't had a real relationship… ever.

Fuck. That's just great. Not only did I break Asher's rule about not having sex with Emma… but I'm the only one she's ever even been with.

I bang my hand on the steering wheel a few times, angry with myself. I know I'm not a grubby teenager anymore, but I still feel like I'm a dirty kid from a bad part of town whenever I think dirty thoughts about Emma.

I'm about to turn on my car and drive away, but at the last second, I see Emma emerge from her house. She's dressed in a fuzzy pink bathrobe and all but flashing anyone who has the good fortune to be looking. She spots me in my car, and makes a beeline straight for me.

I've never seen the expression she's wearing before, but if I had to guess, I'd say I am in trouble. Sitting back, I watch her approach. She doesn't ask anything before she pulls the passenger door open, probably flashing half the neighborhood as she climbs into my Jeep.

For a second we both just sit there, silent. I try to read her face, but I come up empty.

"So…" she says, looking down at her robe. She strokes the bottom of it a bit. "You probably could've handled that better, Jameson."

I look off into the gently rising sun. "And you probably could've told me before we fucked."

She studies me. I can feel her eyes on my face, but I can't bring myself to look at her just yet. I'm ashamed of myself, of how I took her virginity. I'm especially embarrassed of how rough I was with her.

"I didn't think it was a big deal. And honestly, I kind of thought you knew. Like, who would I have given it to?"

She sounds a little puzzled. I blow out a breath, running a hand through my hair. I look at her. "I don't know. I just… I would've done things way, way differently if I'd known."

Emma purses her lips. "I feel like if we'd talked about it back at the bar, you wouldn't have even come over."

I groan aloud. "Yeah, you're probably right. You realize how many ways Asher is going to murder me if he finds out that I popped his little sister's cherry?"

She pulls a face. "I swear, if I hear one more thing about how I am Asher's sweet, innocent younger sister, I'm going to scream. You guys infantilize me too much."

I raise a brow. "Come again?"

"You guys treat me like I'm a little kid!" she protests. I can hear the frustration in her voice. "I'm twenty four years old. And I'm in law school. I might not have as much life experience as you, but I'm a real, actual adult. I am capable of making my own decisions, without my parents or my brother speaking for me."

I can see how upset she's getting. I reach out for her automatically, like I've been comforting her for years. My arm slips around her, and I draw her closer. It's meant to be a one armed hug, but she misunderstands. She sort of launches herself at me, laying her lips on mine.

And I'm ashamed to admit, I kiss her back. Even while I'm beating myself up over the night before, I still feel a special kind of weakness when it comes to Emma. It's the same weakness that brought me to her house last night.

When the kiss ends, I look at Emma. She's got the wispy bits of hair that defy her bun. I take a moment to smooth one back. She grabs my hand, very insistent. She looks at me, her green eyes intently scanning my face.

"Are things going to be weird between us?" she says. "I mean, I still want to learn to surf. And you still have a lot of studying to do. Can we just... still do that?"

I take a deep breath. I can't say no to that. Not with her in my arms, asking me like the question will make or break her day.

I nod slowly. "We can do that."

"Okay." She scoots out of my embrace. "So... I guess I'll see you later, then?"

"Uh huh." I squint into the distance, uncomfortable.

She gets out of the Jeep, closing the door. She stops, then hangs her head in the open side.

"Thanks again. For... you know, unwittingly taking my v card. It was really, really fun."

I don't know how to respond, so I just incline my head. She turns and heads back into her house. I can't help but check out the way that her ass cheeks hang out of her bathrobe as she scurries up the steps to her porch.

Damn. I literally had sex four times in the last seven hours, but I'm still scoping her out like a lovelorn teenager. I shake my head as I start my Jeep, and put it in drive.

20

EMMA

I'm in my last final exam, scribbling the last answer down. I grin foolishly at the finished paper in front of me. I'm done with it, done with the class. Actually, I'm done with all my classes now, as of this moment.

I'm so happy that I actually skip up to the front of the room, dropping my final exam in the basket on the desk. Dr. Smith looks up from his New York Times.

"Finished?" he asks.

"All done." From the pile of papers underneath mine, I can see that I'm not the first. But given that there are twenty more people still taking the exam, I'm not the last one either.

"You may go," he says, already turning his attention back to the arts section of the paper.

I leave the room with a grin on my face. Mouthing, "I'm done!" to myself as I walk down the stairs feels silly but also satisfying. I deserve something really, really good for finishing my first year of law school… and I know exactly what I want.

As I slide into my Mercedes, I pull out my phone and text Jameson. It's been a few days since we spent the night together. I wanted to give him plenty of space, not to crowd him too much. But I feel like celebrating today, for sure.

Hey. I'm in the mood to party. And by party, I mean surf! Are you interested?

I don't get anything back right away, so I head home for a minute. When I pull up outside my house, there are two messages waiting for me. The first is a picture of the ocean, captured just as a wave is rolling in. The second says: *I'm at Breakneck Cove already. You can join if you want.*

That's kind of a weird way to phrase it, but all right. I'm still excited to see him.

I hurry to change into a tiny string bikini, a crop top, and a pair of shorts. I throw my wetsuit into the car, wrestle my new pink surf board in as well, then make the quick drive over to the beach.

Breakneck Cove is close, but it's also kinda packed. The parking lot is jammed full of cars, and people have started parking along the side of the road. Luckily, I see a parking space opening up just as I'm about to enter the lot. I spot J's car as I pull in, and can't help but smile as I grab my surfboard.

I go past the parking lot, taking the well-trodden path down to the sandy beach. I'm taken aback by the sheer number of people on the beach at first. There are kids laughing and playing near the water, their corresponding adults shading their eyes and looking on from the positions further up the beach.

I trudge down the beach. It takes me a minute to find Jameson… and when I do, he is not alone. In fact, he's with three hot girls, trying to catch a frisbee that one of them threw. I stop, worrying my bottom lip.

At least Jameson has a shirt on… because I've seen him without one, and I know what effect it has on women. He's so tall and dashing, with his board shorts and sunglasses. I see one of the girls check him out, not subtly either.

I look at the girls, all gorgeous beach bunny types in string bikinis and shorts. Basically the types of girls I've been trying to imitate. Jameson tosses the frisbee, his whole body flexing for a second. He looks tall and handsome next to the sexy, age-appropriate women he's with.

I am suddenly so jealous that I almost can't stand myself. Jameson looks over and sees me. He raises his hand in greeting.

Perfect. Now I don't have much of a choice. I have to go over there.

I slog over there, hating myself for feeling so much jealousy. After all, it's not like I own Jameson. He can do whatever he wants... I would just rather not see it. Or know about it.

Or even think that it might happen, honestly. I frown.

"Hey," Jameson greets me as I put my surfboard down. He sees my expression, and looks a bit puzzled. "What's wrong?"

"Nothing," I say, shading my eyes as I look out onto the ocean. "Who are your friends?"

"Who, them?" he says, motioning to the girls. He wrinkles his nose. "Just some girls that hang out with the group that I usually surf with."

"Ohhh," I say, relieved. "I mean, that's cool."

He arches a brow. "Is it?"

I blush. I decide to joke my way out of awkwardness. "I just came to learn to surf. You gonna teach me, or what?"

Jameson doesn't look particularly convinced, but he lets it slide.

"Let me grab my board and my wetsuit. We'll go a little bit down the beach, away from the crowds."

He grabs his mint green surfboard, casually carrying it under his arm. His wetsuit he throws over his shoulder. I heft my board and my wetsuit, and we set off down the beach. After a minute or so, the silence feels pretty suffocating, so I try to make conversation.

"I finished my last exam today," I say, hurrying to keep pace with him. Not only is he over a foot taller than me, but I guess he has had a lot more practice walking in the sand.

I've lived by the beach my whole life, but I still have trouble plodding along. He notices that I'm struggling and slows down, for which I am thankful.

"Oh yeah?" he asks.

"Yeah. That means I'm officially on summer break. I can help you study more often. I mean, you know, if you want that."

He looks at me out of the corner of his eye. "Yeah, maybe."

Frustrated by his terseness, I plunge onward. "I was thinking that I could maybe make those flash cards that I mentioned the other day."

He grunts, distractedly looking out at the ocean. The crowds start to thin out here, so he stops and sinks the tail of his board in the sand.

"We should be good here." He wrinkles his nose, but his eyes are hidden behind his sunglasses. "I'm going to go ahead and put my wetsuit on."

"Cool." I put my board down and quickly get out of my shorts and tee, climbing into the wetsuit. I zip it up, and then look at Jameson for further instructions. "Now what?"

He folds his arms, sizing me up.

"Do you remember the steps from last time? Or should we go over them again real quick?"

I bite my lip. "Mmm... maybe practice them one more time?"

He nods. "All right. Lay your board down flat."

I lay my board down, and move to the end. "All right."

"Get on your knees," he orders.

There is a moment of weirdness between us, and I blush. I kneel down at the end of my board.

"Grab the sides, and move onto your stomach."

I do it awkwardly. "Then do sort of a cobra pose, right?"

I push my head up, angling my elbows back. When I look to him for affirmation, I realize that he's staring at my ass, even though it's covered in neoprene.

I cock a brow. "Are you teaching me to surf, or daydreaming about touching my ass?"

He gives himself a shake, narrowing his dark gaze at me. "Quit being mouthy. Now turn your leg..."

He tries to walk me through standing up, but I can't quite get it this time without having him as an example next to me. He frowns and comes over to me, touching my leg.

"You have to move this leg first." He positions my foot. "And then slide this foot forward..."

I shiver a little at his touch. He slowly guides me to a standing position. When I'm finally upright, he's super close to my face, close enough that I could almost turn my head and kiss him. He holds me for a few seconds too long, his hands on my waist.

I slowly turn my head to face him, and he looks down at my lips. I see him swallow. I gently kiss him, but he pulls away.

"Emma—" he begins, shaking his head.

"What, now that you deflowered me, you're not interested?" I accuse, but I keep my tone light.

His look turns black. "Of course not. You know that's not it."

"No?" I ask, arching a brow. Of course I know that isn't his hangup, but it's fun to torment him a little.

Jameson steps back, wrapping his arms across his bare chest. "No. I feel like… Fuck. I feel lucky that you… that I got to…"

I grin wickedly. "Pop my cherry? I hear that's what the kids are saying these days, grandpa."

He gives me a long look. "You know that it's not about that. But there are like a million reasons why we shouldn't fuck again."

"Really?" I say, stepping closer. I reach out and smooth my hand over his chest, looking up at him. I can feel his heartbeat. "When I touch you, I can't think of a single one."

He catches my hand against his chest, holding it tightly. He's got a look in his eyes, like an admission of guilt. "It *is* easy to forget when we're this close."

I push up onto my tiptoes, brushing my lips against his. He makes a low noise in his throat, his hand coming up to cradle the back of my head as his mouth descends upon mine. I part my lips, allowing him greater access. He controls the kiss, his tongue playing with mine. He grips my hair and pulls my head to the side, sucking on a spot on my neck.

When I whimper, trying to wrap my hands in his wetsuit, he makes an anguished sound and pushes me back a step.

"No. This is such a bad idea," he says, a little out of breath. He looks down at me with pleading eyes. "Wasn't one night enough?"

I answer as honestly as I know how. "Not for me, no. Was one night all you needed?"

Jameson's expression is just... angry and lost, at the same time.

"It will have to be," he says. He picks up his surf board and starts heading back toward the parking lot.

"Wait!" I call.

He slows, then turns. "What?"

"I... I'm sorry," I say. The apology sounds lame though, probably because I'm not sorry at all.

He stares at me for a second with those brown-black eyes. "I just... I need some time, Emma. I need to get my head straight, and I can't do that with you close by."

Then he turns and trudges off again, leaving me standing on the beach, watching him go.

21

JAMESON

I'm in my bed, trying to ignore the morning sun as it slants down on me. I have a hell of a hangover from the last three days of hard drinking, and not much else going on in my life.

I have working at Cure. I have surfing. But for the first time, it seems like that's not enough.

Unfortunately, I have an idea of just what would fill that person-shaped hole in my life. Or who, I should say. The hookups and flings that kept me going in the past do less than nothing for me now. I've had multiple chances the last few nights, and yet…

I'm not interested. And I blame most of that part on Emma. Every time I even think about another woman, it's like… it's like other women are in black and white. I know Emma exists in full color, and my enjoyment of the black and white women is just… less than it was a couple of months ago.

I throw my arm over my eyes to block out the sun, and curse Emma. If she wasn't so… pert and bouncy… then maybe I would have a chance of not wanting her again like this.

Foolishly, I thought that having her once would be enough to get her out of my system. The problem is, instead of doing that, I think that fucking her somehow drove her further under my skin.

And of course the fallout from having sex with Emma is on my mind all the time. I swear, if it weren't for the fact that Asher is such a big part of my life, I would say fuck it. I'd bury myself so deep in Emma, she wouldn't know what hit her.

The fact that I am the only man she's ever been with is still astonishing. I don't know the details, the ins and outs of her life that well, but I like to think that she had plenty of chances with other guys… and she chose me. She waited around for *me*.

It's a little mind blowing. That thought makes me oddly proud, at the same time it makes me feel a little ill.

I hear the front door open and close. I'm guessing that's Asher coming home, since he wasn't here when I came in drunk last night. He's obviously getting some action somewhere else, because I haven't seen him but I did see that he rifled through the drawers in the bathroom. He left the giant box of condoms empty, where before there were probably ten or twelve left.

Sex heals all wounds, I guess. Even if the wound is a horrible ex.

Actually, scratch that. *Especially* if the wound is a horrible ex.

I smell something. I take my arm off of my eyes, sniffing the air. What is that, coffee?

Rolling out of bed, I pull on a pair of sweatpants and pad out of my bedroom. I go down the hall and emerge into the kitchen, then stop. Emma is there, with her hair thrown up in a bun, hovering over the stove with a spatula in hand.

I scrunch my face. "How did you—"

My voice scares her, makes her turn and jump out of her skin. She puts her hand over her heart and fans herself with the spatula. I notice that she's wearing a cute little pale pink sundress, the hem of it barely reaching mid thigh. I swallow.

"Good lord, Jameson," she says. She acts like I'm in her kitchen, which is really confusing. "Do you want some coffee?"

I don't move except to fold my arms across my chest. "Do I? What are you doing here?"

"Ummm… Asher gave me a key." She shrugs like it's no big deal. Turning back to the stove, she starts using the spatula on some hash browns. "I um… I mostly wanted to apologize for being so pushy at the beach the other day. So I figured I would come over, make some breakfast, and help you study for the GED."

Emma glances back over her shoulder. I'm sort of befuddled, so I head over to the kitchen table, and pull out a seat for myself. Squinting at her, I sigh.

"Your brother wouldn't like you being here with me."

"Then I guess it's a good thing that I don't live to please Asher." She goes over to the cabinet, and gets down two mugs and a glass. She pours me a glass of water first, coming over to set it down in front of me. "You smell like whiskey still."

I pick it up, not mentioning to her that she's been the cause of a lot of my misery for the last three days. This hangover is half her fault. As I down the water, she pours me a black coffee and then sets it in front of me as well.

She goes back to the stove, easing the hash browns onto two plates, and scrambling some eggs. While the eggs are cooking, she prods them gently with the spatula. I drink a little of the coffee, then get up to refill the water glass.

It's awkwardly silent in the kitchen, mostly just me staring at her ass and her sun kissed legs. I down three more glasses of water, and half the coffee. I don't want to admit it, but the water has already taken the edge off of my hangover.

She opens a plastic container of strawberries, cutting off the tops with a knife.

"I'm going to the bathroom," I say.

She just smiles at me over her shoulder, so I get up and head down the hallway to the bathroom. After a quick piss, I take a few aspirin and brush my teeth. I glance in the mirror and try to smooth down my hair a little bit.

Then I head back to the kitchen. There are two plates of food ready on the counter. She's made toast in the toaster. I catch her putting a fingertip's worth of some kind of jam in her mouth.

We make eye contact, and something dark and unspoken radiates between us. She sucks on her fingertip, which gets me hard as fuck. When she pulls that fingertip away from her mouth, a little smudge of jam is left just above her lip.

"You've got a little, um," I say, gesturing to her mouth. I move closer.

She blushes and wipes at the wrong side of her mouth. "There?"

"No, let me…" I step up to her, and she tilts her head up at look at me. The second I touch my thumb to her lip, I know I've made a mistake. I freeze, my eyes finding hers. It's so easy for her to turn her head a little and kiss my thumb. There is something obscene about her plump lips working over my skin, something I can't just watch.

It's even easier for me to grab her by the waist and haul her up on the kitchen counter, spreading her thighs and bringing us together. My mouth descends upon hers, hungry and demanding.

She opens her mouth and her thighs for me, drawing me in without a second of hesitation. Her hands slip around my neck, fingernails lightly scoring the flesh of my shoulders. I palm one of her breasts, then pinch her nipple, drawing a cry from her lips.

I trail kisses down her jaw, skipping over her neck, and bend down to nuzzle the space between her tits. I feel her legs wrap around me, her heels digging into the backs of my legs, pulling me as close as possible.

I reach down and pull her dress up, finding her bare underneath. I groan as I rip off one of the straps holding her dress up, kissing her newly exposed breast. I know I'm not being delicate with her, but I'm too entranced to care.

She doesn't seem to mind, her head thrown back. She's making these little oh sounds that are killing me, every second I'm not inside her.

Fuck. I need to have her, right this second. But a voice in the back of my head says that Asher could walk in any second… and the voice isn't wrong.

I pick Emma up, with her legs still wrapped around my waist, and carry her down the hall to my bedroom. I get inside, closing the door behind us with a slam, and fall onto the bed with Emma still holding onto me.

Her breath leaves her in a whoosh as we hit the bed, but I use my elbows to keep most of my weight off of her. She kisses me, and I bite her lower lip. She grabs my head and bites me on the neck, which I swear makes my cock pulse.

"Fuck!" I grit out. "You are such a bad girl, Em."

I squeeze one of her tits hard, and she gasps.

"Bad enough to get punished?" she whispers.

"Ohhh fuck," I say, pushing her down on the bed. I look at her for a second, searching her face. "You don't really want that."

She struggles under me, trying to push me off. "Maybe I do."

I bring my hand up to her neck, fitting my fingers around the slim white column of her neck. I apply just a little bit of pressure, making her gasp and writhe beneath me. When I release her, she tries to pull me closer for a kiss. I allow it for a moment, but then I pull back. There is much more I want to do to her.

I move back, kneeling on the bed, and ruck her dress up over her head roughly. I cast it aside, then I strip off my own sweatpants.

Her eyes are immediately drawn to my cock, which jumps at the attention she pays it. She looks up at me, biting her lip.

"Can I taste you?" she asks quietly, seeming unsure.

God, could Emma be any sexier? I reach down and stroke my cock with one hand, nodding.

"You sure you're ready to give head?" I ask.

Her eyes twinkle a bit, and she pushes herself up on the bed. "It's not rocket science, right? You just… you'll have to guide me a little."

"I think I can do that," I say, amused. I look around my tiny room, realizing that there probably isn't room for her to get on her knees comfortably.

But she surprises me by hopping off the bed and kneeling on the floor, looking up at me with complete trust.

"Like this?" she asks.

I get off the bed, taking my cock in my fist. I step closer, and she places a hand on my hip, looking at my dick. "That's… perfect. Jesus, you're hot when you're on your knees like that."

Swallowing, I look down at her heart-shaped face. Her pouty lips part as I guide my cock to her mouth. The second I touch my cock to her lips, the sensitive head probing the wet heat of her mouth, I have to close my eyes for a moment.

My dick twitches, and it takes everything in me not to just bury myself in her hot mouth. I imagine how I would do it. How good it would feel just to put my hand in her hair, to let go and fuck her mouth and throat.

But no. I open my eyes again, breathing hard. She's looking up at me, her lips on the ver tip of my dick, her eyes telling me that she trusts me. I have to remember that.

"Open your mouth a little, and stick out your tongue," I encourage her, pressing the blunt head against her lips. She does, rolling out the velvety tip of her tongue. It caresses the head of my cock, and sends tiny lightning bolts of electricity down to my feet. My toes curl.

"Fuuuuuuck," I whisper. She nudges my hand out of the way, closing her little fist around my cock. I put my hand into her hair as she sinks her mouth down on my dick.

I wince a little as her teeth get the sensitive spot under the head. "Watch your teeth," I warn, tightening my grip on her hair.

She corrects herself, covering her teeth with her lips. She then starts to work her head forward and back, fucking me oh so slowly. I groan as she picks up the pace a little, closing my eyes and leaning my head back.

Usually when I'm fucking a girl's pussy or ass, I'm in a position of complete control. I can stop or slow down as often as I want, which helps me keep from blowing my load before I'm ready. Even with throat-fucking, I am in control more than I am now.

And control is something I desperately need to have, especially now. Especially with Emma. I have to remember that this is only her second time having sex; I can't scare her off of going down by grabbing her and fucking her throat. And as much as I'd like to cum in her mouth, I know that I can't. It's too much.

"Fuckkkk," I hiss. Her mouth feels incredible, it's going to be hard to restrain myself. "Okay, okay. You have to stop, otherwise I'm going to finish in your mouth."

I gently grab her face and push her back. She sits back on her heels, wiping at her mouth with the back of her hand.

"You taste good," she says, her eyes scanning my face. "Did I do it right?"

"Your mouth is incredible." I pull her up, and then toss her onto the bed. "I just didn't want to cum in there, when there are so many other places that call my name."

She giggles for a second. I grab her knees and force them apart, leaning down to kiss her tits. Then I go straight for her pussy, spreading it with two fingers, and licking her clit.

Emma cries out and buries her hands in my hair, her back bowing. I trace figure eights around her clit and dip my tongue into her pussy, loving the scent and taste of her. Just as she gets worked up, her juices flowing, I press her knees up and lick my way around the tiny pucker of her ass.

"Oooh!" she cries, startled.

I kiss and lick it for a second, penetrating her ass with the tip of my tongue. Then I break away, kissing her inner thighs, kissing and biting her breasts.

"I want you to touch yourself again," I whisper in her ear. "While I'm taking you from behind, I want you to make yourself come."

She nods eagerly, and I flip her over. She braces herself on her knees and elbows, showing her pretty pussy and ass to me. I grasp my cock, pressing the head to her entrance.

I lean in, then I stop for a second. "Fuck, I have to grab a condom."

"No, no you don't," she says, a little bit breathless. "I mean, assuming you're clean. I'm on an IUD."

I answer her by leaning over to kiss her on the back, right on her spine. She shivers, and I grasp my cock again. I press my cock to her entrance.

"Touch yourself," I order. She reaches under her body, and starts to play with her clit.

I plunge inside her, and hear her gasp. It feels so hot and so tight that I have to go slow, otherwise I'll come right away.

"Oh my god," she gasps. "Jameson, your cock feels so good."

I grab her hips and use them as leverage while I fuck her, working my cock in and out of her pussy. She begins to tighten her pussy even more as she plays with her clit. I focus, closing my eyes, and try to hit her g-spot every time I thrust.

Finally she bursts, coming with a shout. I speed up as soon as I feel her begin to spasm, letting myself pound into her like a jackhammer. She cries out my name, which has never sounded better.

I feel my cock start to twitch and pulse as I drive home again and again. I feel like I'm coming like a fucking fountain, her pussy milking my cock for everything it's worth.

"Fuck!" I shout. "God damn, Emma."

I catch myself before I slump face first into her back, diverting my weight to fall beside her instead. She doesn't move, she lies on her stomach, facing away from me, her breathing ragged.

I struggle for breath too, but I also feel an overwhelming need to kiss her. I turn her over to face me with one hand, and cup her cheek.

"You okay?" I ask, scanning her face.

She gives me a lazy smile. "More than okay."

I kiss her on the lips, slow and steady. When I pull back, she looks at me with a crooked grin.

"Do you think our food has gotten cold?" she says with a giggle.

"Yep." I pull her close. "Guess we'll have to think of some other way to satisfy ourselves."

She laughs, and I grin. I'm not entirely joking, but I think she knows that.

Or at least she will in a few minutes...

22

EMMA

2007

"Look what I've got!" my friend Karen exclaims, holding up her wrist. She's showing off a new gold bracelet, which totally goes with her white party dress. She's way overdressed for the arcade, but I don't say that. "Isn't it just amazing?"

"It's really pretty," I say, pushing myself further back into the car's back seat. I'm wearing jeans and a top that's printed with a giant butterfly, and I've got my hair twisted up in a bunch of teeny butterfly clips.

Karen looks satisfied with my answer, pursing her lips and nodding. I look at Donovan, our chauffeur, but he is silent as usual. Karen and I are on our way to Asher's 22nd birthday party, or at least the arcade part of the day.

I overheard Asher talking to his girlfriend about the *rager* they're going to throw later in the day. But Karen and I are thirteen, just old enough to have started liking boys and having opinions about clothes.

In other words, we are so *not* invited to the more adult festivities.

"Do you think Asher will like it?" Karen asks, fingering her bracelet. I can tell she isn't really asking for my opinion, especially because she immediately follows her question with a statement. "If your brother will just look at me, I swear to god, I'll like... *die*."

I roll my eyes. Karen might have the world's biggest crush on Asher, but I'm still running a little behind in the crush department. Whatever the magic is that is supposed to make me wide eyed and dumb around boys, it hasn't affected me just yet.

"We are here, Miss Emma," Donovan says, pulling the car to a stop. I peer out the window and find the a plain brick building, its facade a little run down. In fact, aside from the sign that declares ARCADE, you could just go by without knowing what's inside.

I squint out the window. Karen is faster than me, opening the door and hopping out.

"Will you need an escort inside?" Donovan asks.

I smile and shake my head. "No thanks."

"You have your cell phone?" he asks.

I pat my back pocket. "Got it."

"I'll be around the corner, waiting." Donovan smiles at me a little.

"Okay." I start to scoot out of the car, hurrying to join Karen as she pulls open the arcade's door.

I'm immediately engulfed in the sights and sounds of the arcade as soon as I step inside. Screens flash, lights strobe. Everywhere around us there are *ding ding ding*s and disembodied voices saying that I could win!

On top of all that, there are what appears to be a zillion kids, running and climbing all over everything. Karen grabs my arm hard.

"Omigod, where should we go first?" she asks, wide eyed.

"Mmm..." I say, considering. But then Karen digs her fingernails into my skin and squeals.

"Over there!" she says, pointing. I look, and find my brother Asher playing air hockey, bending over every time he hits the puck. I can only see about half of the table, because there's a huge Jeopardy game in my way.

Karen drags me toward Asher. I roll my eyes as we get closer.

"You say hi, and then you introduce me," she orders, pushing me forward.

"Ahh!" Asher exclaims as we approach, raising his hands in defeat. "Good game, man."

I don't recognize the dark haired young man that he is playing with, but he comes closer. I look at his height and his dark eyes for a second. I'm suddenly warm all over and a little short of breath, but I don't know why.

Asher sees me and steps in my line of sight, eclipsing the guy I'm staring at.

"Emma!" he says, coming over to hug me. He wraps his arms around me, surprising me with a genuine hug. "Glad you made it. I had to practically beg our parents to allow you to come."

"Hey, Ash," I say, pulling back to look up at him. "Happy birthday. And... thanks for talking to them about it."

"No problem," he says, ruffling my hair a little.

"Hey!" I say, scrunching my face and putting up a hand to fight him off.

"A-hem?" Karen reminds me impatiently.

Ash releases me, and I wave a hand at Karen. "This is my friend Karen."

Ash just nods to her. "Hey."

I peer around Ash. "Who is your friend?"

The dark haired guy looks at me quizzically. Ash shakes his head. "You know Jameson, Emma. He's only been my best friend for over ten years."

I squint at Jameson. "I do?"

Jameson comes to stand by Asher, his eyes crinkling with humor. "I've been around for a while. You were probably too little to remember a lot of it, though."

I stare at Jameson, feeling a funny tickle in my stomach, like butterflies. "Oh."

All across the building, an announcement comes over the tinny speakers. *"Anyone that wants to play laser tag, please come to the laser tag arena now. Thank you."*

"Yessss," Asher says, pointing his finger in Jameson's face. "Now's my chance to get you back for earlier."

Jameson rolls his eyes. "Yeah, because playing for the third time will really help you beat me."

"I'm expecting you to be tired," Asher jokes.

Karen practically stomps on my foot. "We want to play!"

"Ow!" I say, rubbing my foot. Karen shoots me a death glare. "I mean... yeah. Can we?"

Asher chuckles. "Yeah, sure. Come on."

Karen scuttles ahead, eager to catch up with Asher. I notice that Jameson drops back a little, and I match his slower pace. I surreptitiously glance at him through the corner of my eye. He's really quite tall, with dark hair and dark eyes. He's got very distinguished features, his cheekbones and jawline honed steel.

I notice for the first time that he has a certain heft to his build, a muscular sort of look to him that makes him seem sleek yet strong. I blush when I realize that this is what my mother's secret stash of romances refer to as his *muscular build*.

It suddenly hits me in the face that all the well-thumbed descriptions of the heroes in my mother's books... they all suddenly make sense, looking at him.

"Wanna do it together?" he asks, glancing at me.

I turn eight shades of red. "W-what?"

"Do you want to be on the same team?" He says the words very slowly, like I might be a little dumb or something.

"Oh! Uh... yes?" I say.

"Great." He moves closer, swinging his arm around my shoulders. I almost faint the second his arm makes contact with my shoulders. "We should probably talk strategy..."

He smells so freaking good, I can't even stand it. It makes my whole body tingly. I look up at him, openmouthed, as he starts talking about laser tag.

That is the moment that I know for sure that I am feeling my very first crush.

23

JAMESON

I wake up with the sun already in my face and Emma asleep on my arm. I feel bad even considering waking her up. After all, we were up until the early hours of the morning, fucking like a couple of teenagers. If I'm honest, it's what we've been doing for a week straight. It's starting to be kind of addictive, knowing I have a naked, writhing Emma waiting for me when I get off of work.

Still I have to wake her at some point. Today is Staff Appreciation Day at Cure, which basically means that the store is closed. Asher and I have been planning for months to take everybody to the beach for the day.

I haven't spoken more than a handful of words with Asher in the last week, but I assume that is still the plan. I withdraw my arm from Emma's embrace as stealthily as possible, but her lashes flutter.

"Hmmm?" she murmurs, still mostly asleep.

I get up and find my phone, checking it for messages from Asher. Sure enough, there is a text from him, going to the whole Cure crew.

Redemption Beach, 11 am. Just bring yourselves and your towels. I'll bring the food, Jameson will bring the booze.

There's no other contact, though. I check the recipients list, and find that Emma has been included. That saves me from an awkward conversation about what I'm doing today, I guess.

I head down to the bathroom to brush my teeth. When I get back, Emma is awake and sitting up. She is naked except for the blanket that she clutches to her chest. I see multiple tiny bruises on her neck and shoulders, which I'm ashamed to say are definitely from me.

"Hey," I say, going into my bedroom and closing the door behind me.

She looks up from her phone with a sleepy smile. "Hi."

"So today is staff appreciation day," I say, coming around the bed to stand over her. I reach out for the blanket, and tug it down. She lets me do it, and I'm treated to a glimpse of her dusky pink nipple.

"Yeah, I got the text," she says. She closes her eyes briefly, biting her lip when I shape her breast. When I pinch her nipple, she opens her gorgeous green eyes, surveying me. "It's already ten. You'd better hurry if you're going to actually bring drinks."

I bend down and circle her pouty nipple with the tip of my tongue. She makes a mmmm sound, her hand trailing to my hair, exploring it lazily.

Then she opens her eyes, groaning as she pushes my head away. "I'm serious. You have stuff to do."

I overpower her, kissing her lips for a second. Then I straighten back up. "You're no fun at all."

"You are going to be really bummed when I make you study for the GED later tonight." She scoots off the bed and starts gathering her clothes. "I need to go home and shower and stuff before I head to the beach."

I look at her naked ass as she pulls on panties. "Uh huh."

She sees me looking, rolls her eyes, and throws a shirt at me. "What, you didn't get enough last night?"

I catch her around the waist, cupping her chin and kissing her again. "Enough of you? I honestly don't think that there is such a thing as enough."

She smiles at me, but there is something a little sad in her eyes. "Good to know that you feel that way."

She pushes away from me, and I let her go. As she hurries to pull on a t-shirt and shorts, I'm a little baffled as to what could be the problem.

"Hey, hey," I say, pulling her into my arms again. "You're going to have to tell me what you're upset about. I'm not a mind reader."

She wrinkles her nose. "We'll talk later. You're going to be super late."

Emma pushes me away again, and this time I let her go. She opens the door and disappears, leaving me to wonder what the fuck she's so upset about.

I hurry through getting dressed and gathering sun block, then get in the Jeep. After a quick stop at Cure to pick up all the essential items for drinking, I rush to Redemption Beach.

I pull into the parking lot at 11:05, just in time to see Emma and Asher disappearing down the narrow path that leads to the beach. They are carrying a ton of stuff. I honk at them as I drive by, and they both turn their heads at the same time.

When they quickly look forward again, I'm struck by how alike they look. For a minute there, I was so busy fucking Emma that I almost managed to forget that she is very much like Asher in looks.

I get out of my Jeep just as Gunnar pulls his bright blue Ford Mustang into the parking lot. Gunnar jumps out of his car and hustles over to help me with the several cases of booze, case of bottled water, and cooler full of ice that I drag out of the Jeep.

"Hey, stranger," Gunnar says, picking up a stack of liquor boxes and a case of water.

"Hey?" I reply, unsure what that is supposed to mean.

"I haven't seen you around much outside of work," he says.

I lift my backpack, then pick up the cooler, balancing another liquor box on top. I start toward the beach. "I guess I've been busy."

Gunnar follows. "With what? Or, judging by the mean-looking hickeys on your neck, with who?"

I shoot him a look. He grins, and I shake my head. "Have I ever been the type to kiss and tell?"

"I just figured I would say that I've noticed," he says with a shrug.

I roll my eyes. "Noted."

We chat about the bar on the way down to the beach. As we get closer to the cluster of Cure employees, Emma turns her head and notices us. She quickly looks away, but I catch the secret smile on her face.

I have to admit, my heart beats just a little bit faster when I see that smile. I fucking love seeing Emma smile.

I freeze, there on the beach. Oh, shit... do I love her?

No.

I can't love her.

I *can't*. We've only been fucking for a handful of weeks. It's way, way too early.

Right?

"Hey," Gunnar says, stopping and looking back at me. His expression is impatient. "What?"

There's no time for deep introspection, so I shake my head. "Uh... I just thought I left the stove on at home. But I didn't."

Gunnar gives me a weird look, but Forest comes walking up to us, unwittingly saving my ass.

"What can I grab?" he asks, looking at me and Gunnar.

"Nothing," I say, moving forward. "I think we got everything."

I partially jog the last sixty yards to the group. Maia and Evie are setting up umbrellas, Asher is firing up a little charcoal grill he brought out here, and Emma is looking awkward as hell.

It looks like Asher has invited everyone to join us, even people who work super part-time at the bar. Brandon, Sarah, Alice, and Derek are all digging a hole for another ice chest.

Asher looks up as I put down my chest. I can't see past his Ray-Ban sunglasses, but he is a dick to me right off the bat.

"I didn't think you would actually bother to bring anything," he says, eyeing the liquor boxes and ice chest.

I give him a hard look, ignoring the slight. "I brought everything I need to make a big-ass container of boozy punch. And I brought ice, and bottled water."

"You heard the man! Another hole, coming right up!" Sarah

cries cheerfully. Her bright pink hair and bright yellow bikini are almost as loud as she is.

She directs Brandon to start digging another hole while Alice and Derek heave Asher's ice chest into the first hole.

I settle into making the punch, which turns out great, if maybe a little boozier than I had intended. I pour everything into a big Tupperware jug, and pass out red solo cups. Everybody but Evie and Brandon takes a cup.

"I overdid it last night," Brandon says, waving off my offer.

"Yeah, me too," Evie says, a little too quickly. "Where's the La Croix?"

Maia takes her first sip, and goes, "Whoa! There is... so much liquor in this!"

Gunnar grins and winks at her. "I'll take that as a good sign. Let me top us both off."

Maia rolls her eyes. He drains his red solo cup, and reaches for the jug to refill his drink. Someone busts out a soccer ball, and most of the party moves onto the beach.

I hang back, along with Asher and Emma. Asher is puttering around with the grill, putting on one of the leather aprons we wear at the bar. I refuse to let myself fall into the trap of staring at Emma, so I just sit under an umbrella and sip my punch quietly.

I glance at Asher a few times, but he seems to be deliberately keeping his back turned to me. His little game of finger-pointing has really gone on for way too long at this point, but I'll be damned if I am going to beg for him to listen to me.

"Do me a favor?" Asher asks Emma. "Open the food cooler and pass me that Tupperware full of chicken, will you?"

Emma follows his instructions, wrinkling her nose at the huge container of chicken. "What's that weird brown stuff?"

"I marinated the chicken in teriyaki sauce, because I'm thoughtful." His expression turns sour. "Unlike some people."

I glare at him. "Fuck you, Asher."

He sets the chicken aside, looking grim. "I'm sure that somewhere, someone's fiancee is drunk and vulnerable. Shouldn't you be there to seduce her?"

I sit my cup down in the sand. "I won't tell you again. I did not come onto Jenna. For fuck's sake, I didn't even like her when she was your girlfriend."

"You liked her enough to try to steal her the night before my wedding!" Asher growls.

"Guys—" Emma tries to intercede.

I get to my feet, clenching my fists. "Say it one more time, and I will destroy you."

He rips off the leather apron, squaring off with me. "You ruined my life!"

"That's *enough*!" Emma yells. "I am so sick of you both right now, honestly!" She stands up and comes up to me, pushing me away from Asher. "Come on. He's making the food. You need to take a walk with me."

I glare at Asher, sneering. Emma grabs my face, forcing my gaze down to meet her eyes. It's an oddly intimate gesture, but it does actually force me to calm the fuck down.

"Move," she orders me, giving me a little shove.

Fuming, I take off in the direction of the parking lot. Emma hurries to keep up with my long-legged strides across the sand. I'm furious, ready to rip into anyone who crosses my path.

24

JAMESON

"Slow down!" Emma begs as I hit the wooded trail that leads back to the cars. "You're making me run, practically. I'm not built to run on the sand."

I slow my pace, but don't stop. Instead, I take a sharp left turn, away from the parking lot, and onto a faintly used trail into the woods.

"I want to smash his face," I grit out as I walk along the path.

"He's your best friend," Emma reminds me. "He'll get over it. You both will. This too shall pass, as they say."

"I guess they aren't friends with a complete fucking lunatic," I seethe.

We stumble upon a clearing with a few sagging picnic tables, and Emma grabs my hand, jerking me to a stop. I look at her, the storm within still churning.

"Please stop," she says. "Just... talk to me."

Looking down at her, I feel so much conflict going on inside my head. With Asher, sure. But also with myself, over the fact that I might have real feelings for this girl... the one person that I shouldn't come close to loving.

Emma looks up at me, her eyes scanning my face.

I lunge for her. Her lips are soft and taste wild, yet familiar. I taste whiskey too, although I know it's from me.

Emma makes a small squeak and weakly pushes me away. It

just makes me want her more. When I kiss her a second time, there is no resistance. Instead, she parts her lips and welcomes my tongue against hers.

We kiss for several long moments, my heart beginning to beat faster. Fuck… if possible, I feel even more for her than I did a few minutes ago.

"Emma—"

"Shut up."

In one swift motion, she pulls off her t-shirt to reveal perky tits with hard nipples that begged for my mouth. I descend on her mouth again, grabbing the hair at the back of her head to control her movements. I back her up against a tree, sealing my hand over her mouth.

If she wants to fuck on the sly, I can do that. She's about to find out just how well I can fuck her silently. I kiss her again, holding back my own groan. The feel of my mouth against hers, my tongue as it flicks across her teeth, it is all too much.

Emma slips her arms around my neck, not resisting in the slightest. I reach down for her little shorts, tearing them down and off her legs with ease. When Emma reaches for her underwear to pull them down, I grab her wrists and stop her.

I walk her back until I've got her against the rough bark of a tree. I grab her and drop to my knees, kissing her breasts, her flat stomach. I grasp her ankles, and spread her legs a little. She whimpers.

"Shhhh," I remind her, squeezing her thigh. "If you make any noise, I'll stop. So you'll have to be quiet."

She looks down at me, wide eyed, and nods quickly.

She's in nothing but her panties, which are quickly becoming soaked. I stop, taking a moment to whip her crop top up and over her head, barring her breasts to me.

Goosebumps break out across her flesh as I lean down for a kiss. Her nipples are hard, and I tweak one lightly. She stiffens, but doesn't cry out.

"Good girl," I rumble. I nuzzle into her neck and begin to trail my tongue down her collarbone.

As I move down, she thrusts her chest out, desperate for my

mouth on her nipples. I kiss her breasts and outline her areolas with the tip of my tongue.

I tease her and she makes a muffled moan, clearly frustrated. Finally, when I pull a nipple into my mouth and started to suck, Emma's whole body quivers and stiffens.

I work toward her other breast and she winds her fingers through my hair. I kiss down her stomach, getting on my knees. Emma starts to pant as I near the hemline of her panties.

I kiss her clit through the lacy material and she moans, on the edge of explosion already. When she looks down at the sight of my head between her legs, my big hands wrapped tight on her thighs, she lets out another muffled moan.

I chuckle.

"Please," she whispers.

"Please, what?" I murmur, but I don't look up at her. "Tell me what you want. *Quietly.*"

"Come on," she says, needy. She pushes her center toward my face.

"Tell me what you want," I repeat.

She gripped my hair tighter. "Rip my panties off," she says.

I release her thighs just long enough to oblige. The chill in the air instantly hit the warm wetness of her center, and I can faintly catch the scent of Emma's warm body in the air just around her.

"Now?" I ask.

"Yes!" she insists, writhing.

"And then what?" I ask, and blow lightly on her clit.

"I want you to lick my… my clit," she whispers. A glance up at her tells me her cheeks are on fire.

Immediately, my tongue is on her clit. Without the buffer of the lace between my tongue and her pussy, the pleasure hits hard. She closed her eyes and lifted her head upward.

"What else do you want?" I ask between kisses and sucks.

"Put your finger in me," she demands.

I laugh quietly at her change in tone. I released one thigh and easily slid a thick finger through her wetness, until I slide it deep into her pussy. She moans and presses against it.

"Two fingers," she murmurs, biting her lip. I slip a second finger into her warmth.

Emma opens her eyes and she looked down at me. The power of having her telling me exactly how to fuck her is intoxicating. She starts to play with her breasts, to pinch her nipples.

"Here," she says. She takes my hand that still grips a thigh and brings it to her breasts. I start to roll one nipple back and forth between my fingers.

"Yes," she says, and spreads her thighs wider. I like seeing her like this, naked and splayed out and begging for me to give her pleasure. "My G-spot," she says, her voice shaking. "Hit my G-spot."

I shift a little and try to hit the spongy patch just inside her, making a *come here* gesture. In seconds, she is bucking her hips against my face, covering her own mouth with her hand to keep from making noise.

Emma is so close to coming, I can taste it and feel it. I slow my movements, stilling my hand. I want to feel her come on my cock, greedy as that is. I kiss her inner thigh, and she makes a frustrated sound.

"God, get up here and fuck me," she says, her words angry.

"I think you're starting to like telling me what to do too much," I tease, pulling her down instead. "I'm going to fuck you from behind, and you're going to get off on being silent. Isn't that right?"

Emma's eyes go wide and she nods.

"Good girl." I spend a second shucking my clothes, and then get back on my knees. Emma bites her lip and admires my swollen cock. She reaches for it, but I pull away.

"Uh-uh," I say, shaking my head. "I'm in charge now. Get on your hands and knees."

She gets onto all fours, watching me from over her shoulder. Her ass and pussy are right there, waiting for me. I can't say that I've ever seen a more beautiful sight.

"Fuck me now," she demands.

I smack her ass, hard. "Quiet. Any more noise, and I will punish you."

The excitement I see in her eyes at my words is almost too much. I grip her hips, positioning my cock at her entrance, and bury myself deep inside with a silent shudder.

"Oh, fuck," she whispers. I smack her again, then grab a fistful of her hair.

My length presses hard against her G-spot and her clit begins to throb. As I start to find my rhythm, she squirms.

"Wait," she says, and I stop immediately. "Like this."

Emma pushes me onto my back. She rises onto her knees and perches on top of my thighs with my cock deep within her. At this angle, the pressure against her G-spot is almost too much for either of us to take.

"Harder," she whispers, and I bite down just enough to make her yelp. One of my hands reaches for her clit and the other runs across her breasts.

She's so perfect and tight like this. I start to bounce her while I stimulate every sensual part of her body. I suck at the delicate skin of her neck, needing something to distract me from how fucking good her body feels against mine.

"Emma," I whisper into her ear. "Fuck, you feel so good."

"Make me come," she says, though I can tell that she is already close. I begin to fuck her harder.

"Make me come," she demands again, dropping her head back. "Fuck, Jameson. God, yes. Just like that."

"I'm close," I say, trying to think of anything but how badly I want to spill inside her.

"Make me come with you," she says. "Come inside me."

"Emma—"

"Come with me!"

With a final flick of my slick finger against her clit, I nip at her neck and slam her down onto my cock.

"Fuck, Jay," she cries out, clenching and trembling. The rush of my orgasm explodes inside her, my cock pulsing thick jets of cum. I push her over the edge. She calls out my name and comes hard against my cock.

For a long minute, we just stay like that, breathing hard. Then I hear faint voices in the distance, and she starts to slide off of me.

I pull her close, kissing her hard. "This isn't over."

Emma swats my chest playfully, hurrying to redress herself. I do too, but I never take my eyes off of her. She's just stunning, no matter how much clothing she takes off or puts on.

The voices come closer. As I pull my zipper up, Forest and Maia burst into the clearing, Maia giggling. Forest's hands are on Maia's hips, and Maia has to push him away rather forcefully when she sees us.

"Oh!" Maia says, blushing.

"Uh, here they are!" Forest says. "Err... we came to find you guys."

Emma arches a brow. "You did, did you? Well, here we are."

I look at Forest, and he makes eye contact with me. Something passes between us, brother to brother, and both of us widen our eyes. Forest is definitely fucking Maia, or at least he's trying to. At the same time that I realize what he's doing, Forest is figuring out that Emma and I have been up to more than just talking.

It's quiet for a moment as we give each other long looks. A little *how could you do that with her?* Mixed with some *please don't tell anyone about your suspicions.*

Maia clears her throat. "Um, since we found you guys... why don't we all go back to the beach together?"

I eye Forest. "You girls go ahead. I uh... I need to talk to Forest about... guy stuff."

Maia and Emma both flash me bemused expressions.

"Oh yeah?" Maia says.

Forest coughs into his hand. "Err... yeah. It's okay, we'll catch up with you... soon. Or whenever."

Emma grabs Maia by the wrist, towing her toward the parking lot. "Okay, see you later!"

Maia glares at Forest, but she allows herself to be led away. I watch her and Emma until I'm sure they're gone, then I turn on Forest.

"You can't tell anyone about—" I begin, then censor myself. "Emma and I were just talking."

Forest crosses his arms. "Bullshit."

"I'm serious!" I lie. I never lie to my brothers, as a rule, but just now I don't even feel bad about it. "And what about you and Maia? I saw you, with your hands on her hips."

Forest looks a little embarrassed. "Nothing happened."

We stare each other down for a few seconds, then Forest shakes his head.

"Whatever, man. I just need to know that you're not going tell anybody. Especially Gunnar."

I squint at him. "I won't talk if you won't."

He extends hand to me, and we shake.

"Deal," he says. "Now can we please get back to the beach and never talk about this again?"

"Lead the way." I follow Forest down the path, back toward the beach, lost in thought.

25

EMMA

As I'm lying in my bed, I hear Jameson's heavy steps on the front porch. I sit up. We have some serious stuff to hash out.

When he swings my bedroom door open, I cross my arms and cock my head.

"I didn't know if you were going to show up here tonight," I say.

He closes the door behind him. "And yet, here I am."

"We have to figure out what to say to people," I say firmly, pursing my lips. "Forest and Maia know. It's only a matter of time before everyone else does too, and that includes Asher."

Jameson shakes his head slowly. "I'm not interested in that."

He comes over to the side of my bed. I feel as though I'm being stalked.

"What do you want from me, Jameson?" I ask, a little breathless.

"You know what I want."

"No," I say, and shake my head. "Jameson—"

He closes the distance between us with ease and grabs the bottom of my shirt. With a single hard tug, the snap buttons of my shirt fly open to reveal my bare breasts. I gasp into his mouth, but don't resist. No, I like what he is doing too much for that.

"No bra, huh?" he says as he traces his tongue from my mouth to my jaw. "Looks like this is just what you wanted."

"No, I—"

"Shh," he says.

He hoists me up until my breasts are in his face. My hands rest on his shoulders as he took one of my pert nipples between his lips, sucking slowly. I cry out, feeling each pull of his mouth lower in my body, as though my breast and my clit are connected.

As he lowers me, he kisses his way up my neck to my lips. When he returns my feet to the floor, my head remains upturned, hungry for more.

"Take off your shorts."

I begin to slide the shirt off my shoulders first.

"No, just the shorts. Keep the shirt and boots on. And take off your panties—if you're wearing any."

I look at him, slightly curious, but follow his directions. Jameson isn't surprised to see that I wear nothing underneath the shorts. He sits down on the bed and pulls me close.

The lips of my labia are already swollen, slick with want. Jameson pulls me toward him and kisses my stomach. His fingers gently explore the flesh between my thighs. He dips his fingers into my pussy, causing me to gasp.

Then he withdraws, slowly sucking on those same fingers. "Sticky, sweet, and ready for me. What a good girl you are."

Jameson trails his fingers back down to my pussy, slowly finger fucking me again. He looks me in the eyes as he does it, and when I start getting excited, he bites his lip.

"Look at this," he says, and he shows me how wet his fingers are.

Slowly, he separated his thumb and middle finger. My wetness clings to his fingers, creating a thread. I blush and tuck my hair behind my ears.

I wish I had a little of the confidence I had at the beach, but Jameson doesn't seem to mind my meekness.

"Here," he says, and lies down on the bed. Jameson puts a

pillow under his head. "Sit," he says, and gestures to his mouth. "Right here."

"Jameson, I—"

"Sit."

"I really—"

"Do it right now!" he barks. "Or I'll punish you in ways that you haven't even thought of yet."

I feel my face begin to burn as I approach him, my knees shaking. I straddle his face awkwardly, facing away from him. I am so petite there is no more than an inch of space between my bare pussy and his mouth.

Still, I hold back. I don't lower myself to his mouth, so Jameson closes the distance by darting his tongue into my center. That is all it takes.

I shudder and let out a moan as I lower onto his face. I readjust myself, leaning forward slightly. He directs my clit onto his tongue, and I moan as he swirls his tongue around my sensitive flesh.

Jameson grips my ass as I lean my hands on my thighs and begin to ride his face. He watches my tits bounce overhead, nipples hard, as I occasionally pinch and pull on them.

I close my eyes as I ride his face, with my only thoughts about the sheer pleasure he gives me.

When I shift a little, offering up my pussy, he dives his tongue as deeply inside me as he can. He groans, seeming delighted at the taste of me. As he fucks me with his tongue, I moan and bounce against his mouth.

Jameson grips me ass tighter. His tongue slips its way to the rim of my ass. I cry out his name as he circles the tight bud of my opening.

When it becomes too intense, I lean forward and present my clit to him once again.

"I'm almost there," I say. "Jameson, I'm –"

"Come on my face," he says. He barely gets the words out before I explode in a gush.

"Jameson!" I cry out. "Jameson…"

"You taste so good," he murmurs, his hands wrapped around my thighs to keep me close. I moan and settled onto his face, grinding in slow circles.

"What about you..." I ask, distracted by the feeling of his lips against my inner thigh.

"I don't know. This is pretty nice..." he says lazily.

I shake my head, crawling off of him.

"I want more. I want to feel you inside me," I say. I bend down and run my hand along the outline of his cock through his pants. "What can I do to make that happen?"

He grins, chuckling as he kisses me. Then he gets serious, and I sense the tone change.

"Get on top," he says. He starts unbuckling his belt, shove his pants down. I smile when his cock springs out of his pants. "Ride me."

The ache is almost unbearable. I straddle him, taking his cock and running my thumb along the tip, slick with precum. I furrow my brow as I guide him in, still sensitive from riding his face.

He feels incredible, filling every inch of me until I can't take any more. I watch his face as he slides home, and his expression is damn near reverent.

"Fuck, you feel good," he says, his eyes dark. I withdraw a little, raising myself up again. He grabs me by the waist, pushing me down. I cry out as he fills me up, clenching on his cock.

He makes a strangled noise.

"Stay," he whispers. "Just stay like this a minute."

Jameson is completely inside me, and every instinct within me says to move. To bounce on his cock, to fuck him, to ride him until he fills me with his come. But this, this closeness, it overrode everything else.

My sensitivity vanishes. I put my hands on his chest and begin to writhe, my boots digging into the sides of his legs. I technically do as he said, but it's much dirtier than that.

"Fuck, your body is so perfect. You want to fuck me?" he asks.

I look him in the eye, biting my lip and nodding.

"Are you going to come for me again?"

"Yes," I say, almost breathless.

I continue to press against him, harder and more demanding. He still doesn't let me move, exactly.

Jameson is ready to explode. I can tell by the fact that he's bucking his hips a little each time I grind against him.

"How bad do you want it?" he asks, working his hand into my hair. He grasps it tightly, giving him the illusion of control.

"More than anything," I gasp.

"Ask nicely," he say as he runs his fingers up my thigh, making me shiver.

"Please let me fuck you," I say.

"Are you going to fuck me right, like a good girl?" he ask.

I pause, but only for a second. "Yes."

"Say it, then."

"I'm going to fuck you like a good girl," I say. My juices start to pool around his cock. "Come on…"

"Say it one more time," he say. With all his strength, he presses me down hard onto him. "Tell me who is in charge."

"You're in charge," I moan. "And I'll fuck you right, like a good girl."

"Go on then."

He releases my hips. I go wild, my yelps punctuating by thrusts as I ride him. I rub my clit against his taut stomach.

Just as I feel him release inside me, I let out that now-familiar cry of my own orgasm.

"So good," I whisper, over and over. "Jameson, it feels so good."

I stay on top of him until every last wave of my orgasm has faded. We're still in body-to-body contact when I sit up, looking at him. My voice is soft when I finally speak.

"We have to figure this stuff out," I say.

Jameson kisses me, hard and deep and slow. I can feel him start to get hard while he's still inside me.

"Later," he insists. He grabs my hands, pulling them behind my back. "I need you, right now."

And fool that I am, I let him get away with it. I groan and rock against him, still needing him.

I think that I will always need him.

He flips me over, so that I'm underneath his big body, and we are both lost once more.

26

JAMESON

I'm sitting on my couch, with the television on but muted. I glance at my phone, and find that it's about six in the evening. I left Emma at her house this morning, with the understanding that she would shower and then meet me here.

I actually have a real date planned for us, at a fancy restaurant and everything. I planned something kinky and fantastic for us later tonight, complete with a small army of newly purchased sex toys and restraints awaiting us in my bedroom.

Now, though, I am starting to wonder where she is. And that in itself bothers me... when did I start giving a fuck where any girl was?

That's the problem. Emma isn't just any girl. She's wrapped herself around me, and grown inside me like a weed. Anytime I think about it too much, my heart does this squeezing thing, a feeling that is more than a little bit uncomfortable for me.

Coupled with my thoughts when I was on the beach yesterday, I genuinely have something to worry about when it comes to Emma. She's starting to be a real problem for me.

But she's a problem that I don't want to quit, which makes her doubly frustrating.

As long as I don't let the word L-O-V-E crash into my thoughts again, though, I should be fine. For a while, at least.

When I hear the front door handle jiggle, I'm relieved. It's not that I thought that anything happened to Emma, so much as it is the fact that I'm just vaguely stressed out when she's not in front of me, where I can see her.

I get up and head for the front door, thinking that maybe she's locked out. When I get a few steps from the front door though, the door bangs open to reveal a very, very drunken Asher.

He squints at me. I recoil, expecting him to yell at me again like he did yesterday. But he just trips over his own feet, falling. I step in and catch him, frowning.

He's like about as helpful as a dead fish, snickering like a fool. "I'm *drunkkkkk*."

"Whoa, whoa," I say, staggering under his unexpected weight. It takes me a minute to help him regain his footing. "You are wasted."

He stands up, wobbling his way to the living room. I close the front door, and then head in there too, where I see he has made himself comfortable by sprawling out on the couch.

I walk up behind the couch and cast an eye over him. His eyes are closed, an arm thrown over his face. He could be passed out for all I know.

"Are you okay?" I ask, clearing my throat.

"I have to tell you something," he says, not moving an inch. His words are very slurred.

"Is it why you're so loaded right now?" Asher normally isn't a big drinker. I could count on one hand the number of times I'd seen him this drunk.

"Mmm. Nope," he says, shaking his head under his arm. "Nuh uh. It's about me and Evie."

I still. "I'm sorry?"

"She's a bitch, you know that?"

I'm very confused. "Evie that works at Cure?"

Asher takes his arm off his eyes. "Obv- obvious—"

Then he hiccups. I try to put two and two together, but I'm lost.

"Why is she a bitch, exactly?"

He sighs, sinking down into the couch further. "Exactly. She dumped—" He stops, then hiccups again. "She dumped me. *Me*, Jameson. It's like…"

He makes a frustrated sound. "Who does she think she is, some like… some big time person? Psssh."

"Uhhh…" I didn't even know that they were dating, to be honest. "I don't know."

"That kid is gonna look just like me," he says. "You'll see."

I am so beyond confused. Before I can formulate a question, though, he's onto another topic entirely.

"Jenna's a big ol bitch too. I knew it. I was so mad at you for telling me that, but she was a super crazy bitch. I wasn't even that surprised that she like—" He hiccuped. "Like, she tried to make out with you. She knows that you're like, the most important person in my life, other than my sister. Fucking women, they're all crazy."

There are too many ideas in that single thought. I try to pick them apart, to choose one to focus on.

"I… wait, you knew that Jenna was lying?"

He blows a raspberry. "I figured it out! Well… she admitted it to me."

"Then why were you such a giant bag of dicks for so long?" I say, mystified.

He squints up at me out of one eye. "Didn't want you to be right. Now I'm not married, *and* Evie left me. An all I have is you and Emma to keep me company."

I grow uncomfortable at the mention of Emma's name. "Listen, Ash—"

He sits straight up, pointing a finger at me. "I should be glad to have someone like you on my team, Jay. Like—" He hiccups. "Emma has to be on my team, but you? You're just a good dude. Like, you're loyal, and good. And I'm like, a bastard."

I immediately feel super ashamed of myself, of running

around behind Asher's back with a girl. Emma isn't just any girl to me of course... but she's not just anyone to Asher, either.

How could I let this happen? And with Emma, the only person that Asher claims to care about more than me?

I'm so fucking dead. Stupid, and dead.

Asher struggles to his feet, completely oblivious to whatever internal angst I'm feeling. "I gotta puke."

He launches himself toward the bathroom, and I follow him, feeling all kinds of guilty. I cringe as he vomits for a while, offering towels when he needs them.

I hear the front door open, and I hurry out of the bathroom and into the front hall. I see Emma, showered and smelling like lemons, and I put a finger to my lips.

"Asher is here," I mouth.

Her eyes go wide, and she starts backing out of the house. I put a hand on her arm, motioning for her to wait outside for a few minutes.

I return to the bathroom, where Asher seems to be done throwing up. He's resting his head on the toilet bowl, but I figure he's done.

"Asher? You ready to move into your bedroom, man?"

He nods, mostly asleep already. It takes a lot of effort, but I get him up. I throw an arm around his waist and get him into his bed. He doesn't even notice when I slip off his shoes and turn off his light.

When I leave his room, I go to the front door. Opening it a crack, I look out. I see Emma there, her head down, looking through her phone. Her dark hair spills to her shoulders. She's chewing on her bottom lip, obviously anxious.

I want to go to her, to comfort her. My instinct is to go over to her, grab her, and give her a long, slow kiss.

But what will that solve? Asher will still be her brother. She will still be out of bounds. And don't even get me started on all the other reasons why this thing between us just won't work.

Still, that doesn't make me long for her any less.

I have to break it off. I knew that having sex with Emma was going to get me in trouble, and now here I am. In serious trouble. Still, I *have* to do what's right.

And I will... even if it kills me a little inside.

But not tonight. One last night together won't kill anyone, will it?

She senses my presence, and turns. I open the door.

"Hey," she says softly. She smiles at me, and for the barest moment, I feel hope.

"I'm just going to go get my stuff. Your brother is passed out here, so I figure we should probably stay at your place." I smile faintly, but it feels phony.

She cocks her head at the weirdness in my tone, but shrugs. "Okay."

"Okay. I'll be right back."

I close the door, pausing for a second to lean against it.

I'm going to have to break things off today, and I don't know how I'll do it.

Steeling myself, I go to pack my stuff.

27

EMMA

We fuck until dawn. Jameson seems unusually demanding and possessive, driving both of us to the very edge of sanity. And I am so happy to be with him, to kiss him and hold him… even to be brutalized and punished by him…

I love it. I can't get enough of Jameson, it seems.

Afterwards, exhausted and sleep deprived, I fall asleep in Jameson's arms. I sleep fitfully, tossing and turning. Even in sleep, I know something is wrong. I just can't figure out for the life of me what it is.

As the first fingers of morning creep into thew window, I slip out of bed. Padding down the hall to the bathroom, I sit down and pee. I look over at the little pink plastic chest of drawers that Evie insisted upon when we first moved in.

"It's to keep our necessities in," she said. She dropped her voice to a whisper. "You know, our *lady time* necessities."

I smile at that. She apparently thinks that we need to hide our tampons and pads, in our own bathroom. I get up, going to wash my hands. I turn on the water, run my hands underneath, and then stop.

Turning a little to look over my shoulder, I eye the chest of drawers. It's been a while since I have needed to use anything from inside the chest. How long has it been?

I turn off the tap, wiping my hands on a towel. Doing some math in my head, I realize that it's been... almost seven weeks since my last period. And I've been sleeping with Jameson for... almost a month...

"Shit." I glance at myself in the mirror. "There's no way that... you're definitely not..."

I do the math again, then bite my lip. It could be the stress from finals. Or it could be some kind of secret stress from the pressure not to let Asher know about my relationship with his best friend. That could play a role, definitely.

It could also be nothing.

I open the drawers, digging around, hoping to find a pregnancy test. Of course there are none; both of the women in this house are on birth control, as far as I know.

I bite my lip. I'm probably freaking out over nothing.

Still... I will feel so much better if I take a test, just to be sure. Slipping out of the bathroom, I decide to get to the pharmacy as soon as possible. Better to just put a thought like that to bed, right away.

Once I reach the bedroom though, I know that something is up with Jameson. He's sitting on the side of the bed, totally dressed, his head hanging low. When he looks at me, his expression is tormented.

I close the door behind myself. "Jameson, what's wrong?"

He takes a breath. "I don't want to see you any more, Emma. Or... I don't know. I can't."

My brows shoot up. "What? What are you talking about?"

He stands up, pacing a little in the narrow space beside the bed.

"I talked to Asher yesterday."

I'm taken aback. "I thought he wasn't talking to you still."

"Well, he changed his mind."

I put my hands on my hips. "That's nice, but it has nothing to do with *us*."

Jameson looks at me, his eyes dark. "It was never supposed to turn into this... this... whatever it is, that's between us. I wasn't even supposed to happen at all."

I glare at him. "And yet, it did. Here you are, in my bedroom."

He runs his hands over his face for a second, clearly frustrated.

"I shouldn't have let it happen."

"But you did."

"And I'm trying to undo it!" he shouts. "I'm trying to save us, Emma. Jesus fucking christ, can't you see that?"

"I'm sorry, did you say you were trying to *save* us?" I snarl. "As in, you are trying to save us both? Save us from what?"

"Emma..." he says, clenching his jaw. "We have nothing in common. We're not even remotely connected, except through my *best friend*. And yesterday he reminded me—"

"Reminded you??!"

"Yes! He reminded me of the fact that he's been there for me when nobody else even gave a damn if I lived or died! He helped me when there was no one else. I... I *owe* him, big time."

"That doesn't mean that you owe him your life!" I snap, growing frazzled. "When will you have paid your debt, Jameson? Huh? Five more years? Ten more? Tell me, what is the plan, exactly?"

I see a flash of pain in his eyes. "There is almost nothing I wouldn't give up if he asked me to."

"I'm one of those things, then? You can just... just decide to stop being in a relationship—"

"We were never in a relationship!!" he hisses. "At best, we had a fling. And now, it's *over*."

My eyes fill with tears. He means it. This isn't just another *we really shouldn't* moment.

"You want out?" I say, controlling my voice to keep from screaming at him. "There's the door. No one is stopping you."

His expression hardens. "It's better this way."

"Fuck you," I whisper, looking away as tears start to spill down my cheeks, hot and wet. I wipe them away with the back of my hand. "I mean it. Go straight to hell, Jameson Hart."

He hesitates for a few moments, then shakes his head. "It's better if I do it this way than—"

"Get. *Out!*" I scream at him. "No more explaining! Just go!"

He rips the door of my room open, the expression on his face grimmer than any I've ever seen.

And I'm left in my bedroom, alone, sobbing over him.

What am I going to do?

***

THANK YOU FOR READING "BAD BEHAVIOR". Have you read the Bad Boy Billionaire series? Read Book 1 Now! Lip Service

WANT MORE? READ AN EXCERPT FROM HOW TO LOVE A COWBOY

Pete

I closed the ledger and leaned back into the rich cherry colored leather of the desk chair. I closed my eyes and rubbed my temples, thinking about how much easier things had been when my father was around running things at Killarny Estate. It wasn't anything I hadn't become accustomed to over the years. Being the oldest of the five Killarny brothers, it was expected from birth that I would be the one to take over the day to day running of the ranch. While all the brothers were equal partners in running the ranch, it was I who was the most responsible. Ask anyone. It was also me that my dad had turned to back when my mother, Emily Killarny, had first been diagnosed with breast cancer.

At my mother's request, I took on the additional tasks that my father had usually taken care of. Most of it was business, the sort of thing that didn't capture my attention quite like the quiet, meditative work with the horses, but I knew what had to be done. Most of all, I hadn't wanted to let my mother down.

Emily Killarny was a force unto herself, but she had a kind and good heart, and above all, she loved her children. I was aware that I had a special place in her heart when she had gone out of her way to be the best kind of grandmother she could be to Emma. I'd been dejected and alone, raising a two year old daughter alone after my ex-wife, Kelly, decided one day that motherhood and married life wasn't for her. My parents had been so kind to us in the days following that abandonment, and I would forever be grateful to both of them. My mother had especially done all that she could to make sure that Emma felt safe and loved after her mother's abrupt departure.

Back then my major responsibilities had been tending to the horses, something I still loved and wished I was able to do more of, but being the oldest, and since my father had relocated to Costa Rica, I knew I had to be the one to step up to the plate. My mother's death three years prior had taken a toll on the family patriarch, and after suffering a severe bout of depression, he finally decided to make some major changes. One of those changes included leaving the states and relocating to a warmer climate, leaving the green Kentucky hills behind him in favor of sun and sand. Some days I couldn't help but feel a little jealous of that, but I knew that my heart would always be right here, wherever Emma was.

I opened my eyes again and looked at my computer screen for a moment before getting up and heading for the door, grabbing my jacket on the way. There was still a chill in the air that early in the Kentucky spring and it was invigorating to step out into the morning air, breathing in the fresh smell of new grass and the less pleasing scent wafting from the nearest barn. The smell of manure might not have appealed to everyone, but for me, it was a reminder of home and childhood.

I breathed in the air and made my way over to the stables where my brother Alex was brushing out the coat of a two year old mare.

"She looks beautiful," I said as I came up to stand on the other side of the stall door.

Alex nodded. "Siobhan is quite a looker." He brushed her russet coat to a glistening sheen that caught the early morning sun and made the horse look like a copper penny.

"You think we'll run her next year?" I asked him as I looked over the horse from nose to tail. She was beautiful, but I wasn't sure if she was one of the horses that we would end up taking to the many derbies we were involved in.

Alex shrugged. "Not sure. She hasn't been run that much, and I really think that if we had planned on doing that with her, she should have seen a little more practice at this point in her life. I think she is a great horse, but I'm not sure the derby life is the one for her. However, I do think she is going to give us a lot of talented foals."

Alex was probably the quietest of all the brothers, so hearing him talk this much was a little unusual. The only time Alex had much to say was when he was talking about a horse. Not much for words and usually keeping to himself, he was definitely the most horse whisperer like among us and was more involved with the training of individuals here at the ranch. He was so in tune with the horses that it helped to have his expertise around to help people become accustomed to green horses. While most of our horses were bred here on the ranch, we did keep a group of wild ponies from the Dakotas on one of the spreads of land that was fenced off from the rest. Alex's house was out there and visiting that part of the ranch felt like entering a wilderness. I could see why my parents had given him that parcel when they were divvying up the land to us. It fit my younger brother's personality perfectly, and he was never happier than he was when he was among the wild horses.

"Her mother is Spring, right?" I asked.

"Yeah, and her father was David's Lariat."

David's Lariat had been one of Alex's favorites. A horse that my father had acquired from a Colorado ranch when we were still very young, the horse had been a monster of an animal when we got him. He stood taller than any of our other horses but managed to be faster than almost any horse half his weight. He was a marvel and had produced many of our fastest horses. David's Lariat had died just a year before, but we still had a few of his offspring around the ranch and would likely see his influence in our derby horses for decades to come.

"Well, even if she isn't going to run for us, she's a beautiful girl, and I'm sure she'll give us a few great runners."

"What are you up to?" Alex asked as he put away the brush and stepped out of the stall to join me where I stood.

I shrugged. "Just needed to get out of the office for a little while."

"Already?" He looked at his watch. "It's early in the day. Why don't you hire someone to take care of some of the stuff you don't enjoy? That's what bookkeepers are for, after all. It would give you a break and let you have a chance to get back out here with the horses where you want to be."

Alex was perceptive with more than just the horses.

"Yeah, well, I might do that after the next couple of derbies have passed. I've got too much on my plate right now to hand it over to someone totally new."

My brother sighed and shrugged. "Whatever you say. Just don't be afraid to ask for a little help when you need it."

I gave him a firm pat on the back and continued on down through the stables, past the stalls that housed our many horses. A few of our ranch hands were leading some of the horses out to graze in the pasture, while some of them were headed to the arena and our track for training. As I exited the other end of the massive stable, I saw Emma atop her horse, Saoirse.

"How'dya do, Miss Emma Lou?"

Emma frowned at me, and I could see her brow furrowing under her helmet. I knew she hated it when I referred to her middle name, Louise, but told myself that someday she would come to think of it as endearing, so I kept up the practice.

She tossed her head back. "Saoirse and I just went out for our morning run. I was about to take her back to the stable and then head in for my lessons. Is Hetty here yet?"

I shook my head. "She wasn't there when I left the house, but there's a good chance she's arrived by now. Better hurry on back, you don't want to be late."

My twelve year old daughter beamed at me from where she sat on her horse and headed into the stable before dismounting. I watched her lead her young horse into the stall and couldn't help but notice how much she was starting to look like her mother. It wasn't a bad thing, but I did wonder how Emma would feel as she looked in the mirror and started to notice the resemblance she shared with the woman who left her—and me—behind when Emma was just a toddler.

I walked toward the pasture as I recalled the time directly after Kelly left. It had been a shock to me when it happened, but when I had a little time to think it over, nothing about it was too surprising. We had married straight out of high school, and my parents had been opposed to the match from the start. Kelly's parents were business owners in the nearest town, and ours had been the kind of wedding that made the local papers. Our courtship had been brief — we dated at the end of high school, and because I was an idiot, I had proposed to Kelly not long after graduation. We married and moved into a house here at Killarny Estate and had had a hell of a time for the first couple of years.

Kelly was wild and looking back I could tell she had been just a little too wild for me. It wasn't something I had noticed at the time, and while it was just the two of us, it was easy to forget that we were stepping into a new world that included all sorts of new responsibilities. Back then we would spend our weekends hopping around the bars in town before heading back to the privacy of our house at the ranch and going at it like rabbits. It was no surprise when Kelly got pregnant, and I was overjoyed, but she didn't seem too enthused about it. Slowly she warmed to the idea, and once Emma was born, I could see that she really did love our daughter.

Things were never the same though. Kelly never looked at me the same way, and I tried to encourage her to go see a doctor to see if what she was struggling with was postpartum depression, but she wouldn't listen.

I came home one evening to find all of Kelly's things gone, a note on the kitchen table, and Emma wailing in her playpen. I had picked up my daughter and the note and read the words through tears as Emma sniffled and buried her head against my shoulder. Kelly was gone. She apologized in the letter, said she was heading to California to pursue her dream of being an actress, and that she was going with her friend, Bud.

Bud was the guy she had dated before me in high school, and

suddenly it all started to make sense. We never really heard from her after that, aside from a Christmas card or a birthday present for Emma on the years that Kelly remembered, which were few and far between.

As far as I knew, Emma had no real memory of her mother. It made me sad, but I wondered if it was for the best that she didn't know what she was missing out on. If Kelly had hung around much longer, it would have been more difficult than it already was to get Emma used to not having her mother around.

I had been so grateful to my parents for the support they were during that time, especially my mother. She had done all she could to be the maternal figure in my daughter's life, but she never stopped pressing me to go on dates and get out there again, constantly reminding me that I was still young and there was happiness out there for me if I would just go looking for it.

Her last attempt had been just a few years before she passed away when I had first hired Hetty Blackburn, a local teacher, to be Emma's tutor. The ranch was well out of the way, and it was quite a hike to the nearest school, so I had decided to homeschool Emma. It gave her a chance to be around the horses more and to study at her own pace, which was quite a bit faster than the average elementary school student, according to Hetty.

Hetty was pretty and a very sweet woman. Her black hair and blue eyes were a sort of bewitching combination that was hard to ignore, but I couldn't get back into dating; not then and not now, even though it was 10 years since Kelly walked out. Even if I hadn't already been very hesitant to date, Hetty already had one major strike against her—she knew my daughter.

I leaned against the bright white fence and watched as a group of our horses played together in the dewy field that was filled with clover. The place was even more picturesque than usual in this light. Killarny Estate was really something to be proud of, and I was so glad to have the privilege of being a part of a four generation horse ranch, the largest one in Kentucky, and now, for all intents and purposes, running the place.

One rule I had established for myself was that until I knew I could trust a woman, she would never meet my daughter. And since I wasn't in the mood to start dating yet, nothing had ever made it that far. Sure, I had been with women since Kelly—too many to count—but I was there to get what I wanted and get out. I never went out with anyone that I thought was there for more than what I was because I had more heart than that. But I didn't trust anyone to give me any more than what I was looking for at the moment. It was sex, pure and simple—though rarely pure or simple. I was there for a release, to have sex, hear them scream my name, and then leave quietly. The closest I had ever come to bringing a woman home was the Lawrence girl who I made it all the way back to the ranch with, but we never left my truck. We had made it as far as the pecan grove when I pulled over and had her right there in the cab of my pickup. When we were done, I turned around and drove her right back to her house. But that had been the last one, and that had been a long time ago now.

There was no need to complicate my life any more than it already was and I was certainly not going to bring any of these women into the life of my daughter. She had already experienced enough pain from my poor choices, and I wasn't going to do that to her again.

My middle brother, Jake, came riding up on his stallion and brought the horse to a quick halt a few feet away from me.

"Showing off?" I asked as I cocked my eyebrow at him.

He swung down off the saddle and gave the horse a pat. "This bastard is ready to run!"

Clement certainly looked like he was ready for it. His eyes were wild, but it was clear that he was happy after his morning run with Jake.

"Think about how fast he's going to be with one of the jockeys on him!"

I nodded. "We're taking him to the Waters derby, right?"

"Yup, just a couple of weeks away now."

I noted to myself that I needed to check that out on the calendar. There was still a lot left to do in preparation, and we weren't sure how many horses we would be taking. Clement was certainly on the top of the list, but I knew we needed to have a few backups. Killarny Estate had always been top of the pack as far as producing some of the fastest race horses in the country, but ever since my father had packed it up and gone to Costa Rica, it felt like we had lost some of our edge. I had no idea what it was Dad had that we didn't quite have down yet, other than the forty years of experience. What I did know was that it was crucial for us to win this derby. Things were tight, and if we were going to turn them around and maintain things the way they were around here, or if we were ever going to have any hope of making Killarny the very best again, we had to win the Waters derby.

"You coming?" Jake asked me as he brushed his reddish-brown hair back out of his face and wiped his brow with the back of his sleeve.

I looked at him bewildered. "Of course I am."

He shrugged. "Don't act like it's a given. You haven't been there in years."

"Yeah, well...now I don't really have any choice, do I? Dad is still in Costa Rica, and I don't know the next time he's planning on coming back, so I've got to be there to represent the ranch. And I think Emma would enjoy the trip to Tennessee, so yeah, I'll be there."

"You're not nervous, are you?" Jake winked at me, and I frowned in response.

"Why would I be nervous?"

"Because," he began, pausing to spit on the ground. "Little Sara Waters is going to be there. I wonder if she is going to follow you around like she always used to when we were kids."

I rolled my eyes. "Sara Waters is thirty by now. I am sure she has got better things to do than chase around a nearly middle-aged man with his twelve year old daughter in tow."

"Hey now, don't write yourself off just yet. You're only a year or so older than her, right? I bet she would be champing at the bit to get a piece of a Killarny brother."

I shook my head and started off back toward the stable, Jake following behind me with Clement.

"Then she can have her pick of the other four. Hell, she can have both Stephen and Sam if she wants them." I stopped and looked around. "Speaking of that, where are the twins?"

Jake shrugged as he continued toward the stable. "Who the hell knows. They're out every night of the week. Probably still in bed."

I knew he was kidding about the last thing. If we had been taught anything as kids, it was that getting up early in the morning was the Killarny way.

"Okay, well. I need to go find them. I'll get back to you about the Waters derby. We need to talk about some logistics getting there, but it can wait until later."

As I walked off toward the other barns to locate my two youngest brothers, I couldn't help thinking about what Jake had said regarding Sara Waters. I hadn't seen her since we were practically teenagers. It must have been a decade or so. I wondered what she looked like now and if there was a chance that we'd get some time alone when I was at her father's derby in a few weeks.

GET A FREE BOOK!

Join my mailing list to be the first to know of new releases, free books, special prices and other author giveaways.

http://freehotcontemporary.com

ALSO BY JESSA JAMES

Bad Boy Billionaires

Lip Service

Rock Me

Lumber jacked

Baby Daddy

The Virgin Pact

The Teacher and the Virgin

His Virgin Nanny

His Dirty Virgin

Club V

Unravel

Undone

Uncover

Cowboy Romance

How To Love A Cowboy

How To Hold A Cowboy

Beg Me

Valentine Ever After

Covet/Crave

Kiss Me Again

Handy

ABOUT THE AUTHOR

Jessa James grew up on the East Coast but always suffered a severe case of wanderlust. She's lived in six states, had a variety of jobs and always comes back to her first true love – writing. Jessa works full time as a writer, eats too much dark chocolate, has an iced-coffee and Cheetos addiction, and can't get enough of sexy alpha males who know exactly what they want – and aren't afraid to say it. Dominant, alpha-male insta-luv is her favorite to read (and write).

Sign up HERE for Jessa's Newsletter:

http://jessajamesauthor.com/mailing-list/

www.ingramcontent.com/pod-product-compliance
Lightning Source LLC
LaVergne TN
LVHW011827060526
838200LV00053B/3927